CONQUEST of GREYSTONE VALLEY

Charlie Brooks

grey gecko press

Published by Grey Gecko Press, Katy, Texas.

www.greygeckopress.com

Printed in the United States of America

Design by Grey Gecko Press

Illustrations by Jessica von Braun: www.solocosmo.etsy.com

Library of Congress Cataloging-in-Publication Data
Brooks, Charlie
Conquest of greystone valley / Charlie Brooks
Library of Congress Control Number: 2016935761
ISBN 978-1-9457601-8-1
First Edition

To Quentin and Cordelia,
who have joined Sarah on the adventure

In loving memory of Pat Brooks

One

nother bolt of lightning struck Sarah. It tickled this time. She picked herself up off the ground and grinned. Her hands and forearms had a few burn marks where previous spells hadn't protected her well enough, but she was definitely getting the hang of it now.

A thirteen-year-old girl didn't get a lot of chances to hone her magical abilities. Sarah had wanted to show off on the first day of the new school year, but her mom had been all too clear—no magic in public. She certainly wasn't happy with the ruling, but she couldn't exactly turn her own mom into a frog in retaliation. That type of behavior would almost certainly end with her getting grounded, even though it totally wouldn't be her fault.

Sneaking out of the house in the middle of the night so she could practice her resistance spells was fair game, though, even though it did come with a minor risk of electrocution. She just couldn't say no to the opportunity to go storm-chasing. On top of the defensive magic, it also gave her a chance to practice some other spells . . . such as a sleep enchantment to make sure her mom didn't catch her slipping out of her room.

She dusted off her blue pajamas and ran her fingers through curly brown hair that had become a bit frizzy thanks to the jolts of electricity.

Then she uttered some magical words and picked up the metal bat that served as her lightning rod. She braced herself and flinched slightly as another roll of thunder came in. Her spells were improving, but she was also getting tired. *This next bolt might hurt a little bit*, she thought.

She never got to find out, though, because the storm moved on. Clouds blew by, revealing a crescent moon in the sky. The rain came down in one more furious blast before stopping entirely. With one last rumble of thunder, the storm disappeared completely.

Sarah sighed and started walking back to her house, dragging the bat behind her. Her home sat at the bottom of the hill she had been standing on. It looked large and imposing—too big for only two people to live in, and yet Sarah and her mom had found a way to make it feel comfortable. With the lights turned out, the gray house looked like a moonlit, vinyl-sided castle. The image reminded Sarah of something . . .

"Darn it . . . not again," she said as the thought slipped out of her mind. Suddenly, she couldn't remember what she'd been thinking of.

Moments like that had become all too common. At least once a day, Sarah would start to say something, only to have the thought disappear before they could express it. When she had mentioned it at home, her mom got cloudy-eyed and changed the subject, as though she too had forgotten what they had been talking about.

Shrugging her shoulders, she continued her journey home. The mud made a satisfying squelch between her bare toes with each step.

Tossing the bat at the base of the porch, she got halfway up the six wooden steps to the front door before pausing. As far as she knew, her mom was sleeping blissfully, completely unaware of the storm-chasing episode. But it always paid to play things safe.

She turned around, climbed down the steps, and circled around to the back of the house. Her second-story bedroom had a nice, clear view of the hilltop where she had been experimenting. Come to think of it, she should have taken this approach from the beginning.

"*Vola no fenis.*"

The magic took over almost before she finished the spell. She rose off the ground as though a giant invisible hand was pulling her toward the sky. She had gotten used to heights long ago, so she actually enjoyed the dizzy feeling when she looked at the ground below.

The pull of reverse-gravity stopped as she reached her bedroom window, leaving her hovering. The lock was broken from an experiment that had gone awry over the summer, and she'd continually "forgotten" to tell her mom about it. Without that serving as a hindrance, it was easy to slide the window open as gently and quietly as a shadow in the night.

She closed the window as soon as she got inside. Not a sound except for the occasional creak and groan of the house settling. Now the only problem was her dripping wet clothing, and that was really no problem at all. She whispered the syllables of a quick drying spell, and her body became toasty warm. In less than ten seconds, her pajamas became as cozy and comfortable as if they had just come out of the dryer.

Sarah was about to throw herself onto her bed and record the results of another successful outing in her diary when she heard a click. The noise was quickly followed by more clicks, one after another, starting at the front of the house and heading toward the stairs that led to her room.

Light switches. Every light in the house was turning on by itself.

Having spent the last hour in near-total darkness, Sarah found herself temporarily blinded when the light in her room came on. After the shock disappeared and her vision cleared, she found she wasn't alone.

"I'd say you need some more practice. Wouldn't you?" Her mom's voice came from behind her. Turning, Sarah saw her standing in the corner of the room closest to the window, dressed in her favorite green bathrobe.

"I think I did pretty well," Sarah retorted. "All the spells I cast worked exactly the way I thought they would."

Her mom's eyes flashed. "All of them except one."

Oh yeah . . . the sleep spell. Sarah knew she shouldn't ask, but she couldn't help trying to figure out what she had done wrong with that one. "How did you—"

"Because I'm your mom, and I knew what you had in mind the moment we heard a roll of thunder at dinnertime. I made sure to take precautions before going to bed. You're a very talented girl, but you're also predictable. And disobedient. And, as of right now, grounded."

"Grounded? But I didn't do anything!"

Her mom brushed a lock of gray-brown hair away from her face and stepped forward. "Oh no? Show me your hands, then."

With a defeated sigh, Sarah held out her hands. Her nails were blackened by the storm. And even though she had dried her clothes, the tips of her fingers were still wrinkled from the long exposure to water outside. Nothing left to do now but listen to her mom read off a list of charges.

"Sneaking out of the house without telling me," her mom started. "Trying to cast a spell on your mother. Deliberately getting yourself *struck by lightning*. And you did it all on a school night!"

"Well, when else am I supposed to learn?"

"This isn't open for debate, young lady. If you want to revisit our argument about why you can't use magic in public, that's a conversation for another time. But right now, it's past midnight and you've got a lot of sleep to catch up on."

From one oversized sleeve of her bathrobe, her mom drew a thin, well-polished piece of wood. Sarah tried to remember where she had put her own wand, but that piece of information seemed to have slipped her mind . . . just like the counter to the spell her mom was about to cast.

"*Uermo lia lectus.*"

The spell's effects hit Sarah almost instantly, accomplishing the exact same thing she'd hoped to do to her mom earlier in the night. Drowsiness hit her like a hammer, and she staggered backward. She fell into her comfortable bed and closed her eyes before her head even hit the pillow. By the time her mom turned the lights out, Sarah was fast asleep.

Being a teenage enchantress was hard sometimes. The hardest part, as Sarah repeatedly discovered, was trying to put one over on her equally magical mom.

Two

The nurse gave Sarah a wet cloth to clean the blood from her hand. She was pretty sure it didn't belong to her.

"I never get into trouble," Carrie groaned from the seat next to her. "My mom's going to kill me."

"Hey, at least yours won't turn you into a stone statue and leave you like that all weekend."

Carrie's face paled. "Has your mom done that to you?"

"No," Sarah admitted. "But she could."

The secretary in the reception area just rolled her eyes. Even though the school year was less than a month old, Sarah had already figured out one important fact: she could talk about magic as much as she wanted without anybody taking her seriously. As far as the adults were concerned, she was just a kid with an overactive imagination—and complaints about *that* were something her mom could deal with during parent-teacher conferences.

Carrie blinked her hazel eyes rapidly. Sarah had come to expect the reaction whenever her best friend had to remind herself that she hung out with a secret enchantress.

"Why'd you throw a punch, anyway? Why not turn that boy's skin green or something?"

Sarah dabbed at her knuckles with the wet cloth. Definitely not her blood. "I'm already grounded. I don't need to make it worse. Besides, he wasn't worth a spell."

"Oh, I don't know. I can think of a few I'd enjoy casting on him."

"Ugh . . . I told you, I don't know anything about love potions."

"That's a shame. I thought he was kind of cute."

Sarah rolled her eyes. "You think every boy is kind of cute."

"Well, they kind of are."

Carrie had long blonde hair and a smile that was guaranteed to make her popular with the boys when she got into high school. Sarah was pretty enough too, but boys didn't usually make her want to do anything more than throw a punch. This had given her a bit of a reputation as a troublemaker, but luckily, high school was on its way. As long as Sarah managed to survive this year, she would go to a new school with new challenges—and leave these trips to the principal's office behind.

A door opened, but not the door to the principal's office. Through the entrance that led back to the rest of the school stepped a figure that looked like it belonged in a field scaring away crows. He wore a wrinkled suit that seemed about two sizes too big for him and matched the many gray hairs in his beard. His disheveled hair looked like faded straw that had started to grow mold. Bloodshot eyes and a wrinkled face completed his grim visage.

It was Mr. Daxon, the guidance counselor. Sarah, like most students at her school, recognized him immediately—not because she had ever spoken to him, but because of the wild rumors that flew about when her fellow students tried to guess why he looked so gloomy all the time. Her favorite theory was that a judge had sentenced him to work in the school as some weird sort of community service. Mr. Daxon was still new, but so far, all he had accomplished was to make sure the students got any guidance they needed from someone else.

The dreary old man glanced at Sarah and Carrie, then grunted. He stepped in front of the secretary's desk and cleared his throat.

"Ms. Walker, one of these students has a meeting with me." Mr. Daxon's voice sounded like a violin that was badly out of tune.

The secretary checked her notes, then looked back to the guidance counselor. "Are you sure? I don't have anything written down—"

"It was a recent arrangement." The guidance counselor straightened his back, and it made an audible pop. "Oh," he muttered, "the aches and pains that come with old age." He scanned the faces of both Sarah and Carrie as if he was trying to figure out which one seemed to be more uncomfortable when he looked in their direction. "That one," he said, finally pointing at Sarah. "It should only take a few minutes."

Ms. Walker tapped a pen against her desk. "I don't know . . ."

"She started the fight, didn't she? That means she needs guidance."

"I didn't start the fight!" Sarah shouted as she jumped out of her chair. "That new kid has been after me ever since he came to this stupid school! He's been following me everywhere. He got what was coming."

A moment of silence settled over the room after Sarah's outburst. Carrie looked sick. Mr. Daxon had grown pale, as though he were negotiating with a large bear.

"Okay," Ms. Walker said after an awkward moment. "Sarah's all yours. I'll inform Mr. Martin."

"A-herm-herm-harrum." Mr. Daxon cleared his throat for the third time since he'd brought Sarah into his office. She sat in a comfortable padded chair opposite his desk while he focused his attention on a computer screen in front of him—probably checking her permanent record or something.

"Ahem." He cleared his throat one last time. Then he gave his keyboard an experimental poke, as though he were poking the body of a dead animal. It didn't seem to do anything, but he finally turned toward an increasingly impatient Sarah.

"Computers," he said. "They've been around for days, and I still can't seem to figure them out."

"Days?"

"Or years. One of the two. Who can keep track? We aren't here to debate such matters, Sarah. We're here to talk about you."

"If this is about the fight between me and that new boy, Kay—"

"Oh, no, no, no. Can't stand fighting myself. Never got a taste for the sight of blood. Although, just between you and me . . ." He leaned across the desk and dropped his voice to a conspiratorial whisper. "Who won?"

"Um, well, we didn't really have a winner. I threw a punch, then the teachers pulled us apart."

"Oh." He sat back in his chair with a disappointed frown. "Well, I suppose blood sports in the school halls should be discouraged."

"Um . . . was this supposed to be about guidance, or . . ."

"Ah! Yes! Sarah, I wanted to discuss your future." Mr. Daxon folded his hands together and nodded as though he had just said something very impressive.

"My future?"

"Yes, your future. Have you, um, thought about what you want to do in college?"

"Why college? I'm only in eighth grade."

"Well, somebody with your skills could be a great sorcer—er, secretary. A great secretary someday."

"What did you say?"

They stared awkwardly at each other for a moment that seemed to drag out forever. Did Mr. Daxon know the truth? And if he did, what would her mom say?

As the silence grew more tense, Mr. Daxon moved his hand to cover his mouth as though he were about to clear his throat again.

Doing what she could to stop that annoying noise, Sarah spoke up and revived the conversation. "Why would I need to go to college to become a secretary?"

Mr. Daxon looked crestfallen. "Yes, well . . . ah . . . there are many, er, skills and . . . talents and . . . skills one might . . . hm." He frowned, folded his hands together, and finally abandoned his awkward explanation. "Moving on."

"On to what?" Sarah asked, more perplexed than ever before.

"Why don't you tell me . . . about your father?"

"He's been dead for almost two years now. I went through a lot of counseling." Sarah sighed. "I guess I'm just—"

"No, no," the guidance counselor interrupted. "Let's change the subject to something less dreary, shall we? Why don't you tell me what you remember about Kay?"

"What I . . . remember about him?"

"Yes."

Sarah furrowed her brow. She had that feeling again—something tugging at the back of her brain, like a dream she'd forgotten. Who was Kay? She got an image of a tall, spindly boy not much older than her, holding a wooden staff and a book . . .

No, that was ridiculous. "Kay's just a boy in my class. And for some reason, he won't leave me alone."

Mr. Daxon nodded solemnly, but he seemed a little disappointed by her response. "Well, I wouldn't worry about him." He leaned in close again. "He's not long for this world. None of us are. Really, it's for the best."

Sarah swallowed. "Is he dying?"

"What? No. Goodness me, where did you get that idea?" The guidance counselor checked his watch and touched another button on his computer, which seemed to do exactly nothing. "Well, that's all the time we have for now. Go back to class, don't pick any more fights, and think about your future. Onward, upward, and so forth."

Sarah sat still for a moment, but Mr. Daxon seemed intent on not looking at her. Finally, she got up, left the room, and went back to class.

She had to give the guidance counselor one thing: if getting into another fight meant more visits to his office, she wasn't going to make a fist ever again.

"No, I didn't tell on you," Carrie said as they walked to Sarah's house following the bizarre school day. "But . . ." she shook her head and trailed off.

"But what?" Sarah asked.

"Never mind," Carrie said, her face folding into a deep frown.

"Come on!" Sarah shouted bitterly. "I've had to deal with all sorts of craziness today, from a boy who won't stop bothering me to a guidance counselor who obviously knows more about me than he's letting on. I'm sick of people not giving me straight answers."

"Well, how do you think I feel?" Carrie's shout carried through the cool autumn air and stopped Sarah in her tracks.

"What do you mean?"

Carrie looked like she was trying to hold words back, but after a moment, they came tumbling out like water through a broken dam. "I didn't tell on you, but I wanted to. I mean, why shouldn't I tell the truth? Why should I keep sticking my neck out for someone who doesn't even respect me?"

"What? Of course I respect you!"

Carrie kicked a rock down the street. It skittered to a stop well before reaching anybody. The closest person on the road, an old man in a black coat, was so far away that Sarah couldn't see his face clearly from there.

"You don't really think—" Sarah began.

"No . . . never mind," Carrie said. "I'm just grouchy. And, well . . . worried."

"Worried about what?"

"About where we're going."

Carrie started walking again. Sarah followed alongside her, but her mind took a brief trip into the past. She and Carrie had met in kindergarten, when Carrie was this poor, unkempt, wild thing whose parents couldn't afford her new clothes. The other kids teased her, but Sarah, who was a different kind of wild thing, played with her. That first meeting, she supposed, had colored their relationship in Sarah's mind. Looking at her friend now, Carrie wasn't that dirty-faced, tangle-haired, shy girl she used to be. She saved her allowance to buy herself outfits now. She did her hair carefully every morning. On some days, she even wore makeup to impress the boys. If she had changed that much, where did that leave them as friends?

"Where are we going?" Sarah asked.

"To your house, I hope." Carrie's frown disappeared, and she gave an unconvincing laugh. But whatever was bothering her hadn't gone away—it was just hidden inside for the time being.

"Don't worry about me," she said, smoothing out a wrinkle in the sleeve of her jacket. "I'm just stressed because I thought I was going to get in serious trouble. But as far as Mr. Martin's concerned, I was just an innocent bystander."

Sarah shifted her weight, then decided to let her worries slip away for now. "Of course you're a bystander," she said. "You couldn't get into a fight if you tried."

"Why would I even want to try? Dance recitals are a lot more fun than visits to the principal's office anyway."

"That's all a matter of opinion," Sarah responded.

"What got you to hit Kay anyway?"

"He's a creep. I should have done it a long time ago."

"Maybe, but what specifically set you off?"

"I think he's been stalking me or something. He keeps staring at me when we're sitting near each other in math class, and he didn't even deny it when I told him to knock it off. He said he was still getting used to seeing me without my pajamas on!"

Carrie stopped walking. Her eyes grew large and round. "Whoa . . . you might want to consider, like, reporting that to the police or something."

Sarah touched her bruised knuckles. "If he doesn't take the hint, maybe I will. Then again . . . some of the things Mr. Daxon said seemed odd. Well, they all seemed odd, but I think . . . I think maybe they know something about me."

Carrie grinned, and Sarah caught a glimpse of the wild thing inside. "Do you think they're witch hunters?"

"Don't be ridiculous. There's no such thing as witch hunters."

"Of course there are," Carrie retorted. "It's a matter of history. There were the Salem witch trials—those were the most famous, of course."

"Yeah, but those were hundreds of years ago!"

"Yeah, but where do you think the witch hunters went after the job was done?" Carrie picked up a stick off the ground and started twirling it idly. "They're still out there, I bet, maybe even in our school. Maybe instead of being old guys with buckles on their hats, they're like men in black or something now." She shifted and pointed the stick at Sarah like it was a wand. "They probably read the news looking for strange phenomena and then track down any girls who wave sticks around and say magic words like *aleca leca leera* or whatever."

Carrie was acting like they were telling ghost stories at a sleepover. Sarah wanted to kick her in the shins.

"Come on, knock it off. There's no such thing as—"

The words choked in Sarah's throat. A second ago, they were walking home in bright daylight, but in the blink of an eye, the light went dim as though the sun had already set. A shiver ran through her and her body tensed. Then a pair of small men popped up out of nowhere, and Sarah knew she wasn't the only person in the area who knew about magic.

The two figures looked almost identical. They had chalky skin and pale blue eyes that looked almost ghostly white. They both had greasy black hair and grimy skin. Each had a long, narrow nose that almost resembled a bird's beak, and their hands had jagged, claw-like nails.

"Carrie, duck!" Sarah didn't give them a chance to say anything. After everything else she had been through today, the ability to cut loose and blast a clear danger was something she welcomed.

Unfortunately, Carrie wasn't exactly adept at magical battles. A few real magic words from Sarah brought a hurricane-level gust of wind, but Carrie didn't get out of the way in time. She fell headlong, colliding with one of the dark-clad men.

The other attacker didn't stand idly waiting for another magical attack. He pulled a blade out of his jacket that was almost two feet long and had several nicks and scratches along the blade that suggested it had been used recently. Sarah froze as she looked at the cruel weapon. She could certainly think of a spell to help her. If the other man had a similar sword, though, she wasn't sure she could stop both of them before one of them hurt Carrie.

"Ahem! Ahermhemherrum."

Sarah jumped not because of the noise, but rather because of the unexpected presence of the person making it. The old man in the distance had caught up to them—and he wasn't a random stranger like she had thought. Mr. Daxon's shoulders were hunched and he wore a long black trench coat that was as wrinkled and disheveled as his work suit.

"I hate to interrupt," the guidance counselor said, "but I can't let you harass these two young ladies. They've had a bad enough day as it is."

Neither man responded with words, but the one who had been knocked off balance by Carrie's flying form drew a sword of his own, leaving no doubt as to what he intended.

Mr. Daxon sighed. "What a nuisance."

The guidance counselor reached inside his coat, and Sarah's eyes bugged out a moment later. Crazy old Mr. Daxon drew a broadsword that looked like it had been perfectly polished for just this moment.

Everything that happened afterward seemed to be a blur. The man closest to Carrie grabbed her by the arm, but she twisted away, barely getting free before her attacker could get a better grip. In a split second, Mr. Daxon was upon the silent swordsmen, his own blade moving so quickly that Sarah could barely follow it.

He sliced near one attacker's hands, hitting his wrist with the flat of his blade and causing him to drop his weapon. The other gave up trying to grab Carrie and stabbed at the old man's unprotected flank, but Mr. Daxon shifted and kicked out, catching the assailant in the stomach with the heel of his boot. The silent man finally made a noise, a loud groan as all the air in his lungs came out at once.

Sarah's head swam as she tried to figure out what to do next. She had so many different spells to choose from that she couldn't decide. She had imagined this situation a thousand times, but now that she found herself in it . . .

"Fire!" The call came from Carrie, who dashed away from Sarah so one attacker couldn't be near both of them at the same time. She waved her stick with a trembling hand as one of the men gave up on Mr. Daxon and went after her with his claws outstretched.

It took Sarah a split second to realize what Carrie was saying. Then her head cleared, and she responded.

"Fiera deno partis!"

Carrie waved her stick one more time as though she were trying to shoo the man away, but she closed her eyes in fright as she did so. Just as the attacker was about to grab her, Sarah's spell flared to life. The man's clothes burst into flame, forcing him to drop onto the ground and try to smother the fire.

The victory was shorter lived that Sarah hoped. Overwhelmed by the skill behind Mr. Daxon's attacks, the other man dashed backward until he reached Carrie's trembling form. Sarah's friend opened her eyes just as a clawed hand dug into her shoulder and a blade pressed against her throat. Carrie, caught in a panic, didn't react quickly enough to twist away this time.

Mr. Daxon slowly lowered his sword. Sarah, on the other hand, searched her mind and came up with a spell that could turn the tide of the battle in their favor. Just as she was about to shout out the magic words, though, the man holding Carrie waved his free hand, summoning up a smoky black darkness that enveloped all five of them.

Mr. Daxon yelled and lunged forward, swinging wildly and striking not with the flat of the blade as he had done up until now but with the edge. He would have cut anybody to ribbons had there been somebody there. But both of the attackers had disappeared in the darkness—and Carrie had vanished with them.

As full daylight returned to the area, Sarah looked frantically for her missing friend but found nothing. Only she and Mr. Daxon remained.

"What just happened?" she asked the sword-wielding guidance counselor.

Mr. Daxon tucked his sword back into its sheath in his coat. As he did so, all the energy seemed to leave him. His shoulders slumped, the wrinkles on his face became more pronounced, and he looked as if he had just aged ten years in a few seconds.

His eyes scanned about for some hint as to where the kidnappers had vanished, but all he saw was the small blade one of them had dropped. He picked it up, placed it with his own weapon inside his coat, then turned to Sarah.

"I think," he said wearily, "it may be time for a parent-teacher conference."

Three

Silent, knife-wielding lunatics didn't worry Sarah at all. The fact that they had kidnapped her friend was much more troubling. The fact that her school guidance counselor was a master swordsman who treated this sort of thing as commonplace made her want to scream.

"I'm sorry for this," Mr. Daxon said as he walked briskly down the road toward Sarah's house. "I truly am. I hoped we'd find a way to resolve all of this without the beastly running around and noisy fighting. Oh, the clang of steel on steel may have seemed exciting in my younger days, but now it just gives me a terrible headache. And I didn't stretch properly before the battle, so my muscles will ache for days. I really shouldn't—"

"Mr. Daxon, you need to stop complaining and tell me what's happening!" Sarah shouted. "We need to find Carrie. Is she going to be all right?"

"Are any of us ever truly all right?"

"I was, up until this weirdness started in."

"Really, young one, a girl who summons fire from out of nowhere doesn't have much right calling anything weird." They had reached the steep hill that led up toward the front walkway now, and Mr. Daxon paused to catch his breath. "Your friend is safe for now," he said, striding to the front door of Sarah's home. "Creatures like those don't take prisoners if they don't have a use for them. If we act quickly, we should be able to catch up to them and free her."

"Catch up to them? How? They just vanished!"

"Then I suppose we'll have to vanish too." He rang the doorbell and said no more, as though his words should have made complete sense.

With her nerves frayed from the fight, Sarah saw danger everywhere, and now she turned her suspicions toward the person who had apparently tried to help her. She knew Carrie had been joking about the idea of witch hunters, but what if she had accidentally stumbled onto the truth? After all, what other explanation could there be for a battle-honed guidance counselor following her around? Now her mom was about to open the door and find herself face-to-face with a strange man who had two swords hidden in his coat.

The doorknob began to turn, and Sarah tensed. The words to a lightning spell etched themselves clearly in her mind. If Mr. Daxon so much as reached for his blade, she'd blast him so hard, he'd go right through the living room wall.

The door opened, and as predicted, Sarah's mom stood on the other side. At first, Sarah thought she had just finished exercising, because she still had on the gray sweatshirt she wore when running. However, she wasn't out of breath or sweaty, which meant something had interrupted her before she had a chance to go out.

Her mom looked at Mr. Daxon for a long moment and frowned as though she knew him but couldn't quite figure out where she had seen him before. The guidance counselor himself had an unusual expression on his face that seemed to lie somewhere between nervousness and excitement. Sarah realized that this was the first sign she had seen that Mr. Daxon had any emotions other than depressed and even more depressed.

After an awkward pause, her mom said, "You must be Mr. Daxon. Please come in."

"You were expecting him?" Sarah asked. Had the school called home about the fight?

"Of course. Your friend is inside waiting for you."

Sarah's face lit up. She pushed past both Mr. Daxon and her mom. Carrie was inside! It finally made sense—the whole episode was some sort of weird prank her mom had pulled as payback for storm-chasing last night. Sending illusionary men with swords after her was pretty bad, though. She'd have to find out some way to pay her back for all the worry . . .

Then Sarah reached the living room and stopped dead in her tracks. She felt like her heart was trying to climb out her mouth, taking her stomach with it. It wasn't a trick after all—at least, not a trick her mom was playing. The "friend" waiting for her wasn't Carrie.

It was Kay. The boy sat on the leather couch in the living room with his hands folded and his eyes scanning the covers of the magazines on the coffee table. His looked up when Sarah came into the room, his lower lip still swollen from where she had hit him earlier in the day. He was tall and lanky, wearing blue jeans and a purple hooded sweatshirt that seemed about two sizes too big for him. At least he had taken his shoes off when he came into the house . . . unlike Sarah.

"You?" Sarah shouted.

"Sarah, what's gotten into you?" her mom cried as she walked in to find Sarah speaking the words to a paralysis spell.

A shimmering golden aura surrounded Kay, and he would have found himself frozen stiff had he not said the words to a spell of his own.

"*Contedo al muria!*"

Suddenly, the golden glow covered Sarah instead. Her eyes bulged, and her muscles stiffened. In the space of two seconds, she found herself stuck in place, unable to speak or lift a finger.

"Oops," Kay said, scratching the back of his neck apologetically as he got up from the couch. "That was supposed to protect me from the spell, not reflect it back at you." He scratched his chin, trying to figure out what had gone wrong. "I think I may have reversed one of the syllables . . ."

"Stop. Right now." Sarah's mom stormed to her daughter's side and stood tall, putting forth a commanding presence. "You're going to set my daughter free, and then you're going to explain what's going on."

"Urrm . . . hurngh!" Sarah uttered through clenched teeth. She may not have been able to speak, but that didn't stop her from trying to give Kay a piece of her mind.

"On second thought," her mom said, "explain yourself first, then set my daughter free."

"Mngh!"

"Well, it's kind of hard to explain," Kay said. "We were trying to keep a low profile, but then Sarah punched me in the face and—"

"Sarah! You were fighting in school?"

"Gngh!"

"Oh for goodness' sake . . . *magar otius!*" With a wave of her mom's hand, the glow disappeared and Sarah could move again. "Now you'd better explain yourself, young lady."

"Explain *myself*? You're taking the side of kidnappers!"

"Excuse me?"

"Some people popped out of nowhere and took Carrie! And then I find out this creepy boy can use magic, and Mr. Daxon has swords! Whatever they're up to, we need to stop them right now!"

"I hate to interrupt the screaming and the magic duels, since they're almost certainly more interesting than anything I have to add," Mr. Daxon said, "but we don't have time to waste. Linda, do you recognize me?"

He straightened up, seeming to grow at least six inches in the process. Then he brushed his hair back so it looked almost orderly. For a moment, he looked less like a tired old man and more like a proud warrior whose best days weren't far behind him. His dull eyes flashed, and he gazed deeply into Sarah's mom's eyes as though he were trying to coax something out of her.

Sarah's mom stared back with the same puzzled look on her face that she had possessed when she first answered the door. This time, though, the expression didn't end with her giving up on whatever memory was trying to force its way to the front of her brain. Under the intense stare of the warrior before her, something came through.

"Dax?" She raised a hand to her mouth, holding in a gasp of surprise. "How could I have forgotten you?"

The old man nodded and slumped his shoulders, returning to the tired and disheveled appearance he'd displayed before. "It's been a very long time. I was worried you wouldn't recognize the old wreck of a man I've become."

"Wait, Mom . . . you know him?" Sarah asked.

"You know me too," the old man replied. "I didn't mean to keep you in the dark about it for so long, but I'm not really a guidance counselor."

"Well, duh! That's the worst-kept secret of all time!"

"Yes, well . . . moving on."

"You know me too," Kay said. "Or at least you used to."

"What are you two talking about? Up until the school year started, I had never seen either of you before in my entire life!"

"Yes, you have, darling," Sarah's mom said quietly.

"What?"

"He's a friend—of both of us. Somebody we can trust with our lives, but we've both forgotten him. That means something's very wrong, isn't it, Dax?"

"Something's always very wrong," the old man said. "But to get Kay and I to come all the way here, something is very, *very* wrong."

"Technically, I'm not even supposed to be out of Greystone Valley," Kay said. "Natives aren't usually allowed to leave, but luckily, it seems the rules can get bent a bit since you opened the castle up last year. Still, it was a pretty big risk to take."

"Greystone Valley?" Sarah asked.

"Yes," her mom said. "That's the place."

She walked to a large wooden bookshelf that sat against the far wall of the living room. It was a shelf Sarah hadn't noticed in months, even though it had been in plain sight whenever she entered the room. Her mom scanned it carefully, then pulled down a large leather-bound book. She brought it over to Sarah and opened it. Sarah gasped.

Inside, sketched in careful detail, was a series of pictures and hand-written stories about two adventurers: Sarah's mom and, later on, Sarah herself. Pictures of dragons and giants adorned each page, but that wasn't all. Two images in particular caught her attention: first, an old warrior who looked exactly like Mr. Daxon, leaning heavily on a sword. Second, a skinny boy who perfectly resembled Kay, dressed in baggy purple robes and carrying a staff.

"How could we ever forget?" her mom said reflectively. "We had to have learned our magic from somewhere."

Sarah squeezed her eyes shut as the images whirled around in her mind. She had always known how to cast spells, hadn't she?

No . . . up until about a year ago, she hadn't believed that magic happened in anything but fairy tales. Then, all of a sudden, she had known how to wave a wand and conjure things out of midair. Where had she learned that?

She remembered a land where faeries hid in the forests and dragons flew through the sky. There was a warrior who was afraid of blood and a boy who couldn't keep his spells straight. Someone evil, a warlord, had tried to conquer that land. She recalled her spells crossing with the warlord's steel.

"Greystone Valley." Sarah repeated the name, and it did sound familiar.

"That's right," Kay said. "That's where Dax and I came from, and it's a place that's in a lot of trouble right now."

"No," Sarah murmured. "Those are all just dreams."

"Are they?" her mom asked.

Sarah blinked and shook her head, trying to clear it. Images she couldn't fully understand whirled in her mind. "Why can't I remember it clearly?" she whispered.

"That would be thanks to Melania," Kay said. "She's the one who conquered Greystone Valley, and the best way to keep anybody from stopping her is to make sure the people who pose a threat to her can't remember anything about the world."

"But what about Carrie?" Sarah asked.

"That's a good question," Dax said, "and like most good questions, I'm sure we won't like the answer."

"What happened to Carrie?" a perplexed Kay asked.

"Something kidnapped my friend, and I'm going to get her back!" Sarah shouted.

"Well, we can help you," Kay said. "I'll just bring us all back—"

"Bring us back? Bring us back where?" Sarah felt her confusion give way to panic. "I'm not going anywhere with you people!"

Her mom crossed the room and put her hands on Sarah's shoulders. "Sweetie, it's hard to be sure of anything when we can't remember things properly, but we have to take a chance. I know we can trust Dax. And I know that somewhere in our lost memories, you and Kay used to be friends. If Carrie's missing, we need to start looking for her somewhere. I say we give these two a chance."

Sarah felt herself calm down at her mom's touch and gentle tone. If she was coming with her, it would be okay. After all, who would be able to stop *two* enchantresses?

"It'll be easier to explain all this if we go back to Greystone Valley first," Kay said.

"Are you sure you have the spell right this time?" Dax asked, shooting his companion a skeptical look.

"Of course I do," Kay said confidently. "What are the odds that I mess up the spell twice in a row?" Before the old man could give a response, Kay had drawn a wand out of his pocket and started waving it in the air.

"Wait!" Sarah's mom shouted, stopping him. "Sarah and I need to get ready first. Don't worry—this will only take a bit."

She left the room, and her footsteps retreated upstairs. After a few moments of rummaging around, she came back with two wooden wands and a pair of books with yellowed pages—spellbooks.

"Sarah, honey, remember what I said about not using your magic in public?"

Sarah nodded. "Uh huh. I, um . . . might have broken that rule recently."

Her mom pushed a wand and book into her hands. "Well, where we're going, that rule doesn't apply." She nodded toward Kay. "We're ready now."

The boy spoke some magic words and waved his wand in a large circle. A ripple appeared in front of him, as though the air of the living room had turned to water. Then Sarah saw that the ripple was actually a portal. Through the other side, she saw a castle—large, craggy with age, and definitely familiar to her.

"Here we go," Kay said. He stepped through the portal and disappeared.

"I told you none of us were long for this world . . . and I apologize for whatever beastly trouble will no doubt be waiting for us on the other side," Dax said. He, too, stepped forward and vanished.

"Sweetie . . ." Sarah's mom said. A wave of doubt washed over her face as she suddenly realized the potential danger they were about to step into. ". . . wait."

"Sorry, Mom. My friend, my quest. I've got the power to save her."

Without another word, she ran forward and dove through the magical gateway, ignoring any further objections from her mom.

Four

arrie's head felt like somebody had tried to split it open like a coconut, and the rest of her body felt worse. She tried to remember what had happened after the strange man had taken her captive, but she couldn't focus on anything other than the ache where he must have hit her with the hilt of his sword instead of cutting her throat. Small blessings.

Thinking about fighting and knives sent a chill down Carrie's spine. Somebody had taken her . . . but where?

Finally opening her eyes, she found herself in a place that could almost be considered a palace if it weren't for the bars on the door and windows. The floors were made of smooth, white marble. She lay on a cozy bed with a soft crimson comforter, and an identical bed lay against the opposite wall. A wooden table with tall, thin legs sat in the center of the room and had a clay bowl filled with fruit on top of it. Slipping out of the bed and crossing to the table, Carrie touched one of the apples. It was soft but still fresh enough to eat.

Then there were the bars. The room had two windows, each positioned just above the beds and each small enough that she doubted she could squeeze her shoulders through. Even if she could, thick iron bars blocked any remote hope of exit. The wooden door featured a small barred window and had no knob on her side, making it clear that she was not expected to leave.

Whirling around the strange prison with growing panic, Carrie almost screamed. Then, just as suddenly as the worry had welled up, it disappeared.

"Okay, Sarah . . . just because I was mad at you doesn't mean you get to play tricks like this on me."

No answer. Carrie started to regret her earlier words, but then anger started replacing her panic. She and Sarah were growing in different directions—that was a real concern. She had wanted to talk about it for ages, but she could never find the right time. And when she had finally almost gotten her feelings out, Sarah suddenly decided to make a bunch of imaginary attackers and throw her into a fake prison. It wasn't just a bad diversion—given how badly her head hurt, it was a dangerous one too.

"Sarah, this isn't funny!"

"Who's Sarah?"

Carrie jumped. Somebody else stood on the far end of the room, exactly opposite the door, as though she had been a part of the stone wall up until now.

The girl was about Carrie's age. She had lightly tanned skin, strawberry-blonde hair, and a faraway look in her eyes that made it seem like she was talking to somebody miles away.

"Do you think we can escape?" the strange girl asked.

"Of course we can," Carrie snapped. "We just have to convince—"

She stopped as new suspicions started to form in her thoughts. In the last year, Carrie had seen Sarah perform some pretty amazing feats with her magic. But to create a prison like this on the fly, complete with a cellmate for her, seemed to be a bit much, even if Sarah was upset about the witch-hunter joke.

"Where am I?" she whispered to herself in a voice that sounded far smaller and more frightened than she would have liked.

"We're in the Great City," the girl said. She turned around to look out a barred window. "You can see the clock tower over there in the distance."

"The Great City?"

The girl looked at her as though she had just grown an extra ear. "You're not familiar with it?"

"Let's start at the beginning," Carrie said. "What's your name?"

"Anya," the girl said, forming the two syllables of her name as though each were its own separate word.

"I'm Carrie. Did they attack you too?"

"No. I was told to come here, so I did."

"You let yourself get locked in a cell just because somebody said so?"

"Everybody listens to Melania."

"Who's Melania?"

"Ah," Anya smiled, as though she had just figured out the solution to a puzzle. "You're from far away. We've seen more and more of your kind here ever since Castle Greystone opened. But you were brought here for a reason. You must have magic, yes?"

"Magic?"

A strange light played in Anya's eyes. "Of course. Melania doesn't waste her time with people who have no power of their own."

"This is crazy." Carrie stormed to the cell door and pounded it with her fists. "This has to be . . ."

Her mouth went dry. What if it wasn't a joke? Just before the attack, she had been waving around a makeshift wand and mimicking the strange magical words she had heard Sarah use. Then when the fight broke out, she had called out for fire seconds before a burst of flames had appeared. To somebody who was just guessing, she must have looked like a sorceress. The actual magic words had come from Sarah, but how likely was somebody to notice that in the heat of a battle? Carrie herself had trouble keeping everything straight. For goodness' sake, she even thought she had seen Mr. Daxon of all people waving a sword around!

Slowly, she started to accept the possibility that this wasn't some kind of elaborate prank. And if that was the case, then somebody wanted Sarah captured—or maybe something worse.

All this time, Anya had been studying Carrie carefully, watching her rapidly changing reactions. Now, Carrie took the time to study her cellmate as well. She looked like somebody from the distant past. Her simple brown dress looked scratchy and uncomfortable, and her braided hair probably hadn't been washed for days. She didn't have a watch, a phone, or any other sign of modern technology.

"You're worried," Anya stated matter-of-factly. "You don't think we can get out of here."

"No, I'm worried because even if I did get out of here, I'm not sure I would ever find my way home."

"Focus on one thing at a time." Anya paced around the room until she came to the bed nearest to the cell's window. Reaching under the pillow, she pulled out a long, crooked stick. Carrie only barely recognized it as something that could be called a wand. The magician's wands she thought of were usually black with white tips and capable of sprouting fake flowers. Even knowing Sarah hadn't gotten that image out of her head.

"I know a little of how magic works," Anya said. "You need the words to cast a spell, but even then, it might not work if it's not a spell you've practiced carefully. The wand helps to focus your mind on the magic. Use this." She pushed the wand into Carrie's hands. "Focus on unlocking the door. Then we can escape."

Carrie almost threw the wand to the floor. *I can't use magic*, she wanted to scream. *I'm not who you think I am.*

But those words didn't come out. Instead, she just stood, blinking in confusion.

"What's the matter?" Anya asked. "Why won't you set us free?"

Anya had appeared out of nowhere—Carrie was sure she had been alone when she woke up. And if the girl really was a prisoner, how did she produce a magic wand so easily? True, she could have snuck it in under her dress or hidden it through some other means, but it seemed just as likely that this was some sort of trick.

No, not a trick—a test. Anya wanted to know if Carrie could use magic.

Why don't I just tell the truth? she asked herself. *What do I owe Sarah, anyway?*

Her supposed friend didn't seem to care if she got Carrie in trouble by fighting Kay for some dumb reason. But if this wasn't a trick, the stakes were higher than a trip to the principal's office.

"Why did Melania capture you, Anya?"

The girl looked startled, as though a bee had just landed on her shoulder. "What?"

"You said she's only interested in people with power. What's your power?"

Anya blushed and looked at the floor, almost as though she was ashamed of herself. "I . . . I don't know."

Carrie placed the wand on the table and shrugged her shoulders. The less her captor knew about her, the better.

"I'm not interested in escaping right now," she said.

The blood left Anya's lips. "What?"

"You managed to sneak this wand in here. Good for you. That means I can use my magic to escape whenever we need to. That's the ace up our sleeves. But we're going to need a plan for what happens once we get out of this cell." *And I'm going to need to know whether I can really trust you*, she added silently.

Anya sat cross-legged on the bed. "But . . . you do have magic, right?"

Carrie put on her most confident smile, picked an apple out of the fruit bowl, and took a bite.

Five

"Quick! Everybody count your fingers and toes!"

The portal led them somewhere dark, the only light coming from a small, glowing bulb Kay had created at the tip of his wand. At least, it had been a wand a moment ago—now it was a wooden staff as tall as he was. And he wasn't wearing a hooded sweater and blue jeans anymore but was instead dressed in baggy purple robes and a pointed hat that almost fell down over his eyes.

Mr. Daxon—or rather, Dax—was also dressed in a more medieval-looking outfit, his coat replaced by a simple gray tunic and his broadsword now resting in a scabbard at his hip. The smaller sword he had taken from the kidnapper had no sheath but was tucked into the other side of his belt. Now, both blades touched the ground, because the first thing Dax had done upon getting through the portal was sit down and frantically start pulling his boots off so he could count his toes.

"Why fingers and toes?" Sarah asked.

"Come on, Dax," Kay said. "How many times do I need to tell you I don't make the same mistake twice?"

"No," the old warrior groaned, "you make brand new ones."

"Only sometimes." Kay turned toward Sarah so he could answer her question. "It's a little hard to explain this whole portal-between-worlds thing. The magic's pretty new, since Greystone Valley used to be sealed off. To get through the portal, I have to get a clear picture in my head of what we'll look like on the other side. And, well . . ."

"I had eleven toes for eleven days," Dax said. He counted again, just in case. Finally satisfied he had the right number of digits, he put his boots back on.

Just to be on the safe side, Sarah checked her hands to make sure she had the right number of fingers. Then she noticed that her clothes had changed too.

"Why am I in my pajamas?"

"Um . . . why wouldn't you be?"

"Do you want to get punched again?"

"Hey, hey! No need for violence!" Kay raised his staff defensively. "Last time you were here in the valley, that's how you arrived. I thought maybe it was ceremonial travel garb or something."

"Relax, honey." Sarah looked in the direction of her mom's voice and found that she, too, was wearing blue pajamas. "We're here now. We might as well do the best we can with what we're given." She opened the book she had brought, flipped through the pages, and found a spell she wanted. *"Arium en hiaas."*

The clothes on Sarah's back twisted and changed like they were alive. In a few seconds, they had turned not into her school clothes, like she was expecting, but a set of gorgeous green robes that fit her perfectly. A leather satchel at her side gave her a place to put her wand and spellbook. Sarah's mom soon created a similar outfit for herself.

Kay took a step back and blinked rapidly. "Wow."

"What?" Sarah asked.

"I just . . . wow. It's just really hit me. I mean, two Emerald Enchantresses! I don't think this has ever happened. I don't even know where to begin!"

"You can start by telling us where we are," Sarah said.

The doors were the only reason Sarah could identify their location as a building instead of a deep cavern. The four companions were in a hallway that stretched as far as she could see, and doors lined both sides of the stone-walled corridor. The structure had at least one balcony, with more possibly lurking in the darkness overhead. Each door was made of sturdy wood and had a heavy brass knocker on it. If there was any way of telling them apart, Sarah didn't know what it was.

"This is Castle Greystone," Kay said. He started walking down the corridor, and the rest of the companions followed him. "It was closed until your last visit here. The wizard who created it had even laid down rules that said natives of the valley weren't allow to travel through the doors. But since then . . ." He paused and shook his head, still beaming at the fact that he had a pair of living legends right next to him. "The rules have changed. Magic gets out now and then, which is why you two can cast spells in your own world and why Dax and I were able to reach you. The only ones who can't leave now are the dragons, and that's mostly because nobody wants to challenge the word of Adlin the Dragon Queen."

"Dragons?" Sarah asked. "There are dragons here?"

"Well, sure. There's just about everything here."

Sarah touched the knocker to one of the doors. An image of what lay on the other side flashed through her mind. It didn't open to a room, but rather to another world. She saw neon lights everywhere, tall buildings that seemed to touch a smog-filled sky, and cars that flew through the air. She pulled her fingers away, and the image disappeared.

"Do you remember this place, Mom?"

Her mother nodded. "I'm starting to. This castle is named for Greystone Valley, the world between worlds."

"Exactly," Kay said. "Hundreds of years ago, a wizard saw that the world was changing. People were growing more cynical and didn't believe in the old fairy tales anymore. Instead of letting all those wonders disappear, he created this valley. It has the power to pull in special people and strange creatures from other worlds—"

"Including the Emerald Enchantress," Dax said, placing a hand on Sarah's mom's shoulder.

"And, many years later, her daughter," Kay continued, pointing his glowing staff at Sarah. "A daughter who opened this castle, which gives access to all the other worlds Greystone Valley touches. That means the valley's magic can get out too. I think that's one of the reasons why the memory magic affected you all the way in your world. But don't worry—you'll remember everything soon enough. Memory charms can hide thoughts away, but they can't make them disappear entirely. Now that we've broken through a little bit, the rest will start to come— especially once you see the valley for yourself."

The hallway was wide enough for all four of them to walk side-by-side, but Kay took the lead and Dax brought up the rear, his hand on his sword. Both of them looked at each door that they passed suspi- ciously, as though they were expecting some kind of monster to jump out from behind it at any moment.

As they walked, Sarah did indeed feel the return of old memories, memories that explained a lot of little things from the past year that hadn't made much sense before. "I'm starting to get it . . . but why is Carrie mixed up in all this?"

Kay picked up his pace as he saw a pinpoint of light in the dis- tance. Sarah guessed it must have been the castle's exit.

"I'm still trying to figure that out," the boy said as he nearly tripped over his own robes. "But it's got to be connected with Greystone Val- ley's current troubles. See, whoever controls the valley controls the paths into and out of a million different worlds. And right now, a very dangerous woman has taken over."

"Her name is Melania," Dax said. "And she's the one responsible for erasing your memories." He sighed deeply. "Although you'll get used to forgetting things once you become as old and doddering as I am.

"The two of you, well, you're kind of legends here—even if everybody only knows you as the Emerald Enchantresses. And with the castle opened, she knew there was a possibility of you returning to the valley and setting things right. That's sort of what heroes like you do, after all. Nobody notices when you get grounded or called into the principal's office—all they know is that you show up when you're needed and then disappear when the job's done. But it's a lot harder to come to the rescue if you can't remember ever setting foot in the valley in the first place. Melania has some strong magic of her own, and she cast a memory charm on you and everybody who ever knew you."

"Then how did you remember us?" Sarah asked.

Kay turned around, beaming. "Dax and I got clever," the boy said as he walked backward. "We erased our memories *before* Melania could do it."

"Don't make it sound intentional," Dax said. "We did it because we got lost in the mountains and Kay cast the wrong spell when he was trying to find a way down. Luckily, Kay's magic was temporary . . . unlike Melania's."

"Yeah, well . . . sometimes, it's about results, not intentions. Besides, I got us down from the mountains, didn't I?"

"Oh, yes. You gave us the knowledge we needed to find our way . . . at the cost of remembering our own names." Dax sighed as he continued trudging along. "Not that I wouldn't mind forgetting my problems for a little while longer," he moaned. "My old bones are aching from all this walking."

"Don't worry, we're almost—yeargh!" Not watching his step, Kay tripped and landed with a hard thud on the castle's stone floor. "We're almost there," he said.

Sarah helped Kay to his feet. "So that covers almost everything, but why didn't you just tell us that right away? Why try—and fail, I might add—to blend in with the rest of the people at school?"

Kay started moving again but walked at Sarah's side instead of in front of her. "Well, going to you wasn't actually our first plan. We thought we could overthrow Melania all by ourselves—you know, be the heroes of Greystone Valley and whatnot. But it turns out . . . swords aren't going to do the trick. But we didn't find that out until *after* we tried. So she knew we knew that, but we didn't know if she knew we knew she knew that, but if she *didn't* know that we knew she knew—"

"Get to the point!" Sarah and her mom yelled at the same time.

"Right. Well, we thought it would be best to lay low outside the valley for a while. And . . ." Kay sighed as a strange look that was somewhere between sadness and frustration washed over his face. ". . . you know, it's really hard to figure out what to say to somebody who you think of as a close friend but who doesn't even recognize you!"

Dax sighed and nodded.

Sarah put a gentle hand on Kay's shoulder. "Maybe you could have started with, 'Please don't punch me in the face.'"

Kay laughed a little and nodded. "I don't know if that would have stopped you, but maybe you would have taken a little muscle off of it. You hit pretty hard. Oh, good. We're finally out of here." The boy waved a hand over his staff, and the light went out. They reached the opening of the castle, where the brightness of day welcomed them.

"There's something I still don't get," Sarah said before they left the castle. "If Melania had made us forget everything and she knew we weren't a threat, why did her goons attack me? And why capture Carrie? She's never even been to this place."

Kay furrowed his brow. "That's a good question. Maybe she knew we were getting close to restoring your memories and panicked. Or maybe she's got another plan we don't know about."

"It wouldn't be the first time we've been left in the dark," Dax said. "And it certainly won't be the last."

They stepped across the threshold and entered an area that seemed to wake Sarah up out of the half-dreaming state she'd been in. The autumn air was crisp and fresh, carrying with it the smell of pine needles. The sky was a solid blue with only a few clouds in sight. Snow-capped mountains loomed on the horizon like a great wall. Next to Castle Greystone, which itself was so scarred and craggy that it looked almost like another mountain instead of a true castle, stood a gigantic statue with its arms outstretched toward the sky. The statue looked human, but it had the hooves and head of a ram and was easily fifty feet tall.

Sarah's mom stepped ahead of the group and surveyed the area, taking an especially long look at castle's open door and the gigantic statue in front of it. "Well," she said, "things have changed since I've been here last." She turned to look at the rest of the group. "You've changed too, Dax."

Dax blushed and seemed ready to say something that might not have sounded as depressing as normal, but he snapped back to normal when a low rumble echoed through the surrounding mountains. The old warrior drew his sword.

The companions couldn't see the newcomers until they cleared the trees and hills in the area. When they did, Sarah recalled them through her returning memories as beast-men. Like the statue, they had hoofed feet, humanlike bodies, and animal heads—though maybe calling them beast-*men* was a bit of a stretch, since about half of the group seemed female. They wore simple brown clothing and armor that had lost its sheen years ago. No two of them seemed alike—Sarah could see horse, goat, ram, and mule heads among them.

Taking a quick count of the creatures, she estimated that there were about twenty of them in all. Half of that number ran forward with axes, swords, and clubs in hand. The other half held back, drawing bows and taking aim. The bows made Dax's swordsmanship almost useless and meant that the three wizards in the group needed to hope they could cast a spell faster than the beast-men could let go of their strings.

"Well," Kay said. "This definitely wasn't the sort of homecoming I was hoping for."

Despite the danger, Sarah grinned. A fight—and a chance to let loose with her spells for a change—felt like just what she needed right now.

Six

A beast-man with a boar's head ran forward, stopping a few feet away from Dax's waiting blade. The rest fanned out in a circle around the companions.

"You," the boar-man said, "are trespassing."

"What?" Kay shouted. "This is Castle Greystone. None of you own this place!"

The apparent leader of the beast-men puffed out his chest. "We don't care about the castle. But out here, you have come too close to our holy site." He gestured at the gigantic statue of the ram-man that loomed just outside the castle's doors.

Despite the fact that he had at least half a dozen archers pointing arrows at his chest, Kay refused to back down. "You sided with the war-lord when he tried to take over this valley. You should realize there's nothing holy about that statue! Why don't you—"

"Kay," Sarah's mom said. "Hold your tongue for a moment. Please." Lifting her arms up, she held her open palms where everybody could see, as though she were surrendering. "I'm sure we can discuss this like civilized people. My name is Linda . . . and you are?"

The beast-man grunted. "Calydon. But you are mistaking this for a negotiation. Too many humans have been sneaking about here lately.

You've already pushed us to the mountains because a few of us followed the warlord. I won't let you push any further!" His thick, guttural voice raised almost to the level of a shout, and several of the beast-men who followed him gave yells of agreement.

"We aren't looking to push anything. In fact, if you put your weapons down, we'll part ways in peace."

The boar-man walked close enough to Sarah's mom that his hot breath blew back her hair. His long tusks twitched as he scrunched his face, deciding whether to take the woman at her word. He shook his head slowly and tightened the grip on his spiked club. Sarah's mom stood tall, not backing down an inch.

Sarah wasn't about to let the monster take a swing at her mom no matter what. With the attention of the beast-men focused away from her, she pointed her wand downward and moved it in a small circle. Focusing her mind, she imagined the ground itself bending to her will. And with just a few magic words, that's exactly what it did.

"*Creas terri arum,*" she whispered.

Calydon had taken a step back from Sarah's mom, seemingly impressed with her courage. Then, human and beast-man alike tumbled to the ground as the earth began to shake—except for Sarah, who expected it.

"You want a fight?" Sarah shouted. "Let's see who's trespassing now!"

Her statement didn't really make much sense. But then, fights didn't need to make sense.

While the beast-men picked themselves up off the ground, Sarah prepared another spell. Except for her storm-chases and other late-night adventures, she hadn't had much of a chance to use her magic lately, but she had never stopped studying. Now, every spell she had carefully memorized came rushing into her brain, just aching for a chance to get out.

She needed to deal with the weapons first. Words came tumbling from her lips, and she barely heard them through the rush of excitement that pounded in the ears. With a wave of her wand, she made each sword, axe, and bow wielded by the beast-men feel like it weighed ten times as much as it did. Instead of retaliating, the beast-men who'd gotten back onto their feet were left struggling just to lift their weapons.

Confidence surging through her, Sarah kept the pressure on with more magic. A wall of wind in front of her so any beast-men who did manage to lift their bows would find their arrows blown away before they could hit her. Booming thunder so they wouldn't be able to hear any orders Calydon screamed at them. Bursts of fire so as to burn anybody who came near. Twenty beast-men? No challenge. They should have come at her with fifty or a hundred. She'd still take them all.

Something zoomed by her head so closely that it nearly sliced her ear. She turned around. She'd forgotten about the beast-men behind her. Too bad for them—now she remembered they were there, and they'd missed with their one shot.

Magical energy was still crackling between Sarah's fingertips as she raised her hands. What next? Maybe she'd blast them with ice and see if she could freeze any of them solid.

"Sarah, stop!" Her mom's voice cut through the haze of battle. Reluctantly, Sarah turned around.

Two of her companions had regained their feet following the earthquake. The third hadn't. Dax was bleeding through his tunic. The arrow that had whizzed by her a moment ago—the one meant for her—was sticking out of his side.

She only had to look at the old warrior's sword lying on the ground to realize what had happened. His blade had been pinned under the weight of the same spell she'd used to stop the beast-men. While he tried to force it off the ground and enter the fight, the arrow had caught him off-guard.

Sarah froze. She knew spells that could turn people invisible, call lightning out of the sky, and turn solid rock into fragile glass. But she didn't know any spells that could close a wound.

Kay and Sarah's mom had both rushed to Dax's side, letting their guards down in the process. With them distracted and Sarah stunned for a moment, the beast-men had time to recover. They forced their way past Sarah's spell, lifting their weapons slowly at first but then regaining control of them. Calydon gave a snort and raised his hand, giving his archers the signal to prepare to fire.

"Thank you," he said to Sarah's mom, "for reminding me that the honeyed words of humans only lead to ambushes and lies."

Silently, Sarah cursed herself. She shouldn't have let up. Dax would be okay, she was sure of it. But now, all four of them were about to serve as target practice for the beast-men.

Then a loud roar echoed through the sky before the beast-men could strike. A burst of fire tore through the air less than a second later, leaving a burn mark in the ground right next to some of the archers.

Arrows flew skyward, but none of them came anywhere close to hitting the dragon. Sarah had to squint even to see it—it appeared as nothing more than a tiny white speck in the otherwise clear sky. How it managed to spit fire with any accuracy from that high up was beyond her.

"This is our holy ground!" Calydon yelled. "We won't let it go without a fight!"

Calydon's determination didn't seem to rub off on his followers. About half the force beat a hasty retreat down the mountain paths they'd come from. It was strange, Sarah thought, that they seemed willing to stand and fight against a sorceress gone wild, but even a glimpse of a dragon left them running away with their tails between their legs. But then, there had been thousands of tales told about gruesome dragons, while everybody's memories had been erased when it came to Sarah's exploits. It would take a lot of work on her part to build up that kind of fearsome reputation. She saw that as a challenge worth accepting.

"Get over here!" Her mom waved frantically, beckoning her to come to Dax's aid.

Sarah dashed through the chaos to join her companions. Dax looked worse than she'd first thought. His face had gone pale, and his teeth were clenched in pain. She helped him to his feet, and his limbs trembled with the effort of standing.

"It's okay," the old warrior gasped. "I'm fine. Never felt better."

"Oh my gosh," Sarah said, taken aback by the warrior's unusual optimism. "He must be dying."

Her mom pointed to some bushes a few dozen yards away. "We can get some cover over there. Hopefully, the dragon and the beast-men will forget about us while we regroup. Sarah, help me support Dax. Kay, follow close behind us and use your magic to cover us if you need to."

"No, I can do that!" Sarah yelled.

"Haven't you done enough already?"

Sarah felt as though her mom had just hit her in the chest with a large, flat rock. Any more words of protest got knocked out of her, and she immediately followed her mom's orders. She'd seen her mom angry, frightened, and sad before. But she had never seen pure disappointment directed at her like this. She would rather have been struck down by one of the beast-men's arrows.

Luckily, the dragon did a fine job of distracting the remaining foes. The companions made it to the bushes and tried to lay Dax down gently. However, the old warrior had already lost quite a bit of blood and crashed in a heap as soon as the others tried to lower him.

Dax's eyes closed, and his lips drew tight, forming a single horizontal line. His breath came in labored gasps, and it seemed like each inhale took more effort on his part. Sarah grabbed then arrow shaft to pull it loose, but her mom slapped her hands away.

"Leave the arrow in. We don't want to remove it until we have a way to dress the wound and stop the bleeding."

"Bleeding?" Dax moaned. The old warrior opened his eyes just long enough to look at his blood-stained tunic. Then he shuddered and almost fainted away completely. "Never . . . could stand the sight of . . . blood."

"You're going to be okay, Dax," Sarah said. "Right, mom?"

"I hope so," her mom said, although she didn't sound very confident. "We need to figure out a way off this battlefield first."

"Don't worry," Kay said, peering out from the bushes. "Our backup is doing a good job."

"The dragon's your backup?" Sarah's mom asked.

Realization dawned on Sarah as she remembered some of her old adventures. "Yeah," she said. "Of course the dragon's his backup."

The bursts of fire were coming less frequently, but it didn't matter much. The only beast-man who hadn't retreated was Calydon, and he was shaking. Then, when the dragon finally dropped from the sky and landed on the ground, the boar-man's whole attitude changed. Rather than cower in fear, he burst out laughing.

The creature which had seemed so far away was really only a little larger than Sarah's hand. What everybody had thought to be a trick of distance was a mouse-sized dragon that happened to spit fireballs.

The white-scaled creature landed directly in front of Calydon and growled fiercely. Unlike her roars in the sky, which had sounded like they came from a much larger beast, this noise sounded more like the mewl of a kitten. Ignoring the threat, Calydon raised his club to squash the creature. The dragon tried to spit fire in retaliation, but only a small smoke ring came out. It seemed to have used all of its flame up while in the sky.

Kay glanced at the two enchantresses. "Can you two take care of Dax yourselves?"

"Why?" Sarah's mom asked. "Do you have a spell that can help the dragon?"

"Nah. Spells tend to backfire." He scooped up a handful of dirt and leapt out of the bushes. "At least mine do."

Calydon swung his mighty club, but he found his target much harder to hit than he expected. What the dragon lacked in size it made up for with speed and grace. However, breathing so many frequent fireballs had definitely left it out of breath, and it seemed like only a matter of time before the boar-man got in a lucky shot.

Kay threw his handful of dirt in the air, but it didn't seem to accomplish anything. Not a single speck got in Calydon's eyes, and more landed on the dragon than anywhere else.

Kay, though, seemed to be quite satisfied with his work. He hopped backwards quickly, letting his ally land in front of him as Calydon began to bear down. The dragon, with dirt still in its nose and eyes, began sniffling. Then it sneezed, unleashing an even larger fireball than before. The burst of flame caught Calydon point-blank, burning his club to cinders and lighting the beast-man's clothing on fire. With a howl, the boar-headed creature fled in the same direction his compatriots had, frantically beating at the flames as he ran.

"Good job, Keeley," Kay said. "But how did you know we were here?"

The creature flapped her way to the top of Kay's head and perched on the wide brim of his hat. "Actually, Keeley didn't." The dragon spoke in a high-pitched female voice that reminded Sarah of a time at a fair when she and Carrie had breathed in helium from some balloons. "But she stayed close to the castle, yes she did, and she noticed the beast-men coming near. They didn't look like they were going to cause any trouble, but Keeley decided that if Kay and Dax did come back early, she had better make sure—"

The dragon's bright green eyes suddenly widened as she realized something. "You *are* back early!" she cried. "Does that mean . . ."

Kay nodded and gestured toward the bushes.

Keeley flew in low, twittering with delight. Crashing through the twigs and leaves, she ran into Sarah with enough force to knock her off balance. Surprised that something so small could hit so hard, Sarah found herself looking into the eyes of a very excited-looking dragon.

"Sarah! Keeley has missed you so much! Tell all about your . . . oh my . . . oh no!"

The dragon's joy disappeared as she saw Dax, whose wound was still being tended to by Sarah's mom. And Sarah realized that she might have lost one of her old friends before she even fully remembered him.

Seven

Sarah's mom refused to let any of the companions move from the spot, even as Dax struggled to reach his feet. Without hesitation, she tore the bottom hem of her robe to create some makeshift bandages. Within moments, the green cloth became stained red.

"When it comes to getting shot with arrows, Dax, you're lucky."

"It certainly doesn't feel that way," the old warrior moaned.

"I don't think the arrow hit you deep enough to pierce a lung or any other major organ. As long as you're not coughing up blood, I think you'll live."

"Blood . . . why does everybody keep mentioning blood?"

"Um . . . because you're covered in it," Sarah said.

"Don't remind me! *Please* don't remind me!"

"Kay, do you know much about herbs?" Sarah's mom asked.

"Of course I do!" the boy said confidently. "Wizards make excellent herbalists!"

"But Kay," Keeley said, flapping around his head like a hummingbird, "what about that time when—"

"Of course," Kay added quickly, "I could probably use a little bit of help looking for . . . um . . . whatever it is you need me to find."

"No need. Sarah and I can look for the herbs."

"And Keeley will help!" the dragon shouted.

"Of course. Are you squeamish about blood, Kay?"

"No, that's Dax's thing."

"Please," the wounded Dax hissed, "stop saying the B-word."

"Okay." Sarah's mom tore another strip of cloth from her robe, leaving her calves exposed. "Use these to soak up the, um . . . red stuff. Apply pressure to the wound, but don't press down too hard. Sarah, Keeley, and I will be back as soon as we can." She glanced at Sarah, then focused on Keeley as she provided instructions. "We're searching for small bushes that look like they have pine needles on them. The sap should help make sure Dax's wound doesn't get infected, and the moss that grows near them should make a good poultice."

"Just leave it to—" Sarah began. But her mom walked right past her without listening.

Sarah kicked hard at a rock, knocking it into the underbrush. "It's not my fault," she protested to the air. But even she didn't feel entirely convinced.

The crashing sound in the undergrowth ahead of them could have been more beast-men, but it was most likely Keeley, who dove head-first into any thicket she came across. Sure enough, when Sarah cautiously stepped into the ferns among the fallen trees, the tiny dragon burst into view, her white scales smeared brown and green from the dirt and moss she'd rolled around in.

"Keeley's changed a lot in the year you were away, hasn't she?" she asked cheerfully.

The dragon perched on her shoulder. Sarah scratched her gently under the chin. She studied Keeley carefully—some of her memories were still hazy, but to Sarah, the tiny dragon looked the same as she always had.

"I know," she said at last. "You've, uh . . . grown so much."

Her diminutive companion puffed out her chest proudly. "Thank you for noticing. Keeley has grown a whole inch. And she's learned how to roar!" She let out a short but very loud roar that left Sarah's ears ringing.

"Yes . . . thank you for that." Sarah winced before kneeling down to poke through some weeds in hopes of finding the herbs her mom was looking for. Once again, though, she found nothing. Leaving the plants behind, she heard her mom investigating a hedge nearby. "Keeley, can you go ahead and see what you can find over that rise?"

"Of course!" Keeley took off but then circled back around to Sarah's shoulder. She nuzzled against her cheek, then took off again.

Sarah walked quietly toward her mom, who was focused on digging through a patch of moss. "I'm sorry I let that happen to Dax," she said. "I should have cast a defensive spell first."

"No, Sarah. You shouldn't have cast any spells at all."

Sarah stomped her foot and dug her heel into the dirt. "I needed to do something. Otherwise they would have killed us all!"

"If you had let me talk just a little longer, I would have been able to avoid a fight entirely."

"How can you expect to avoid a fight when you're dealing with twenty armed monsters?"

"Monsters?" Her mom stopped focusing on the plants and glared at Sarah. "What makes somebody a monster?"

"Uh, when they've got animal heads and start waving weapons around, they're monsters."

"And what do you think we looked like from their perspective?"

"We were just four people coming out of a building!"

"Walking through an area they consider special, with one of our companions holding two swords and the rest of us all obviously capable of casting spells. They weren't hunting us . . . they were threatened by us."

"Well, the feeling was mutual, then."

Sarah's mom ran her hand across her face in frustration. "I told you to wait before you jumped through that portal. I should have held you down and made you stay at home. You're just a child."

"Excuse me? You wouldn't have been able to stop me. I'm the Emerald Enchantress too, and I've already proven I can save this valley without you!"

"You're also still grounded—don't think I've forgotten about that."

"You're still trying to threaten me with that?!"

Her mom sighed and rubbed a hand across her face. "Look, sweetie," she said in a calmer tone of voice, "your power is impressive, but it doesn't do us any good if you don't learn restraint. If you can get past an obstacle without starting a fight, you've already won."

Sarah felt blood rush into her head. It wasn't because she was really that angry—it was because she was starting to get the sneaking feeling that maybe her mom had a point. But she wasn't ready to admit defeat quite yet.

"Maybe I'd be more restrained if I was allowed to cut loose once in a while at home. Even when no one's looking, you're always trying to force me to hide who I am. I can't use my magic in school, I can't use it at home . . . now I wind up in a place where I *can* finally use it, and you're still telling me not to!"

Sarah stormed into the wilderness, not paying attention to her direction. Her mom followed quickly, unwilling to even give her a moment of peace.

"Sarah, you need to stop being so—"

Her words stopped abruptly there. Sarah half-expected to hear her storming off in frustration, but there was no sound of footfalls in the leaves around them. Her mom had just stopped making any noise at all.

She turned around and felt her heart do a somersault. Her mom lay face-down on the ground.

"Mom?" The word came out almost as a whimper, then was followed up with a cry of "Mom!" as Sarah rushed toward her.

With a groan of effort, she turned her mom onto her back so she could at least breathe without sucking in a nose full of dirt. There was a bit of a grass stain on her forehead, but otherwise, she seemed to be sleeping peacefully, complete with a blissful smile on her face.

"What's going on?" Sarah muttered. Then she noticed a needle sticking out of her mom's neck. No, not a needle. Squinting and leaning closer, it was a tiny arrow with violet feathers that were almost too small to see.

Sarah sat up with a shock. The sight of the arrow had touched upon one of her recently regained memories, and she knew the danger they were facing. She shouted the words to a defensive spell before she even saw the next projectiles approach, blowing two of them away with a gust of wind. Only after she had defended against the surprise attack did she see her assailants. When she stared right at them, they looked like little green fireflies. But she knew that if she glanced at them out of the corner of her eye, they would actually be tiny people, even smaller than Keeley. They were the mischievous fey of Greystone Valley.

"Listen to me, you annoying little bugs! We're not trespassing, and we're not interested in playing any of your stupid games. If you so much as think of doing anything to me or my mom, I swear I'll set this whole forest on fire!"

"Oh my . . . we wouldn't want that, would we?"

The voice was accompanied by a groaning sound, as though the trees were about to collapse and arguing amongst themselves which way they should fall. Rocks shook and roots started to move, shooting out of the ground and twisting into a roughly humanoid shape. The two tiny faeries which had shot Sarah's mom twittered and danced excitedly at this new development. Forgetting the risk of getting shot by an arrow that might put her to sleep, Sarah focused all her attention on the strange root-creature that had just appeared before her.

The roots shuddered and then became more flexible, bunching together and taking the rough form of a woman who stood just a little taller than Sarah and had a pronounced hunch. The treelike creature swayed from side to side but didn't seem to have any feet with which to move. The two faeries darted to her side and landed on her wooden shoulders. The roots around the makeshift face twisted once more, leaving deep, empty sockets where the figure should have had eyes. In another moment, a pair of pale white lights in the shape of two crescent moons emerged from the sockets and looked at Sarah. The tree-formed face scrunched up and formed into a toothy smile as it saw her.

"Lovely little Linda. You look as young as the day we first met."

"I'm not Linda," Sarah said. She raised her wand defensively with her left hand and pointed toward her fallen mother with her right. "She is."

The tree-creature shambled forward, leaving a raised trench in the earth where the roots pulled away from the ground. Bending her head, she smiled in a matronly way. "Of course it is. Well, this is truly, tantalizingly terrific. I didn't know I had another grandchild."

"Grandchild?"

"Not literally, of course. Great-grandchild, at least. Or maybe even great-great. It's so hard to keep track, especially since I'm a spirit now instead of a person with a real body."

"That's ridiculous. My mom's grandmother is . . . hm." Sarah considered herself well educated, but she hadn't really spent much time studying her own family history.

"How do you think you mastered such magnificent magic, my dear? It wasn't Linda, and it wasn't you, but one of your family was my very own daughter, born here from a little tryst between myself and the Wizard. Alas, we had to send her away during the Dark Times. It was the Dragon Queen's idea."

"The Dragon Queen? You know her?"

"Of course I do. I hated the idea of losing my grandchild at first, but the Dragon Queen was right—you always do come back in one form or another. My Emerald Enchantresses. Such a lovely title. I absolutely adore alliteration, don't you?"

"Emerald Enchantresses? But I thought everybody in Greystone Valley forgot about us."

"Almost everybody—and the spell even reached through the open doors of Castle Greystone to touch your mind, my dear." The tree-creature crossed her arms over her body as though she were hugging herself. "That's the type of magic that only Grandmother Sabrina can teach. But I wouldn't let anybody cast a memory charm that could be used against herself."

"You taught Melania her magic?"

"Oh, no . . . she already had plenty of her own."

"But you just said you taught her."

"I did, didn't I? Memories are magnificently mysterious things, aren't they?"

Sarah turned her head so she could see the faerie creatures on Sabrina's shoulders out of the corner of her eye. Catching a quick glimpse of their true forms, she noticed they had their bows lowered. As long as she could keep Sabrina talking—even if her words didn't make any sense—she was safe.

"Melania erased our memories too. We almost didn't find our way back here."

"Yes, my dear. That's what she thought would happen. But somebody as elderly and experienced as I knew to have faith in you. Whenever Greystone Valley is in danger, the enchantresses come to help. And this time, I met with a startling level of success even I didn't suspect—two of you! That means one can have your harrowing, heroic adventure, and the other can remain here with a grateful grandmother."

"I won't let you—" Before Sarah could finish her sentence, Sabrina flung an arm in her direction. In a split-second, the roots that formed the spirit's hands lashed out at Sarah like wooden whips. Her arm went numb as one root struck her wrist, forcing her to drop her wand. Another root wrapped around Sarah's neck, tightening just enough to make it apparent that Sabrina was in control.

"Let me? My dear, nobody *lets* me do anything. I take what I want, and all I want now is one of my grandchildren back. Don't worry . . . it won't be for very long. After a few years, I'll let you go on your merry way."

"I can't go without my mom for a few years!"

"Please don't struggle dear. Just enjoy some soothing sleep."

The firefly forms glowed a brighter green. Tilting her head, Sarah saw them level their bows at her, preparing to put her to sleep like they had her mom. Forced to admit that she didn't know what to do, Sarah opted for the only other thing she could think of.

"Keeley! Help!"

The call for help gave Sabrina pause, and her tiny fey archers hesitated for a moment. In the next instant, a dragon's roar echoed through the forest, followed by a burst of flame that caused the spirit to drop Sarah and throw up her arms in defense. Sarah grabbed her wand and threw herself against her mother protectively. Keeley landed in front of the two enchantresses and snarled, wisps of smoke coming out of her nostrils.

"Leave Keeley's humans alone or she will show you why fey fear the dragons!"

Sabrina wavered. For a second, it seemed like she was going to fight, even though Keeley's fire would almost certainly make short work of her wooden hide. But then she blinked her crescent moon eyes and smiled.

"Quentin, Cordelia, you may leave for now." She brushed her hands against her shoulders, and the two faeries took flight, darting away into the sky. "My, but I had forgotten how many faithful friends you attract. Call for me before you leave, my dears. If nothing else, you can regale me regarding your recent deeds."

A gale rushed through the area, kicking up dirt and leaves in a furious cyclone. As it did, the roots returned to the ground, and Sabrina disappeared.

As soon as the wind died down, Sarah's mom opened her eyes. "—bull-headed. Why am I lying on the ground?"

"You fell asleep!" Keeley said with a giggle. She took to the air, seemingly forgetting the danger the companions had just been in. "Come along now, Sarah and larger version of Sarah! Keeley has found the herbs!"

"'Larger version of Sarah?'" Sarah's mom sighed in frustration as her daughter helped her to her feet.

"Don't worry, Mom. We'll teach Keeley your name eventually."

Her mom touched the side of her neck and grimaced as she pulled out the tiny fey arrow that had put her to sleep. "Before we do that, why don't you explain what happened?"

Their argument all but forgotten, Sarah gave her mom a big hug. "I, um . . . was learning about our family tree."

Eight

"**I** think you might be a liar."

Carrie took another bite of the apple and chewed it slowly as Anya made her accusation. She kept the fruit in front of her face so her cellmate couldn't see the slight tremble in her lips.

After she finally swallowed the bite, she took a deep breath and forced a smile that she hoped looked nonchalant. "What makes you think that?"

"I gave you a wand," Anya said as she tapped the stone wall impatiently. "Why wouldn't you use it to escape? It's the simplest of spells . . . unless you don't know how to use magic in the first place."

There seemed to be something sinister behind that accusation, like Carrie was supposed to be ashamed of the fact that somebody had kidnapped her by accident. Carrie wanted to throw the apple at Anya, but that was the sort of aggressive thing Sarah did. She could handle things in a better way . . . she hoped.

Summoning up all the self-control she could muster, she walked to the table and placed the core of the apple neatly next to the fruit bowl. Then, with the utmost control, she walked with the grace of a dancer back to the bed, sat down, and smoothed out her clothes. Calm, collected . . . ladylike.

Then she took a breath and tried to talk through the problem with grace and civility . . . but it turned out that her anger wasn't quite as controlled as she had hoped.

"Listen, you. I just got my noggin scrambled when some monster with a sword bashed my head in. I wake up in a world I don't recognize with a cellmate who hasn't stopped nagging me from the moment I woke up. If it's so easy to get out of this cell, you do it. But since you obviously can't, you're going to have to wait until I'm good and ready to escape. Got that?"

Anya pressed her back against the wall, her face pale.

Carrie sighed. So much for self-control. If Anya was a possible ally, she needed to be nicer to her. Even if she was part of a trap, yelling at her would accomplish nothing. Well . . . almost nothing. At the very least, that outburst left Carrie feeling a little better.

"Sorry," she said, going back to her sweeter disposition. "It's just been a crazy day, and I'm not quite myself. Part of me thinks this might all be some sort of practical joke, and my head aches, but . . . hm."

"But what?" Anya asked.

Carrie touched the lump on the back of her head. Just a bit of pressure on it made her wince. That was when she decided that she needed to rule out the possibility that Sarah had played some sort of trick on her. There was no way Sarah would ever let things get so out of control that she'd leave bruises like that.

"I need to meditate," Carrie announced.

"Why?"

"It'll give me a chance to think things through. It's, uh . . . something wizards do."

She had to assume this was a lie—she couldn't imagine Sarah meditating if her life depended on it.

Nonetheless, she crossed her legs, closed her eyes, and did her best to pretend that Anya wasn't there.

She didn't know what this would accomplish at first. She just needed some time to think without Anya needling her. But as she focused more and more on her deepest thoughts and feelings, she found herself confronted with one major truth. It wasn't a way out of her cell—that remained a mystery for now, just like the question of how long she could get away with pretending to be an enchantress. Instead, it was something she'd been grappling with long before the shadow creatures had taken her: the fact that her friendship with Sarah was probably over.

It hurt her even to think it, but she couldn't see any way around it. Sarah had shared an incredible secret when she'd told Carrie that she knew magic, but it was a secret that had driven them apart. It was another thing that made Sarah special, even superior. All of Carrie's interests seemed frivolous and flighty by comparison. How could she stay friends with somebody who made her feel so inferior?

And all that didn't even touch on the fact that she'd apparently been pulled into another land entirely. Sarah's world of magic had made Carrie feel helpless before, but now she really was helpless.

As she realized that her ponderings weren't getting her any closer to escaping her cell, Carrie frowned and opened her eyes, looking toward Anya again. But Anya had vanished.

Carrie got out of bed and tapped the walls experimentally, trying to find a secret passageway through which her cellmate might've fled. She scanned the floor and ceiling for trap doors but also found nothing.

Anya had handed her the wand, but Carrie hadn't physically touched her. Could she have been some sort of ghost or illusion?

Although she now had to deal with yet another thing she couldn't explain, at least it gave her a moment to check her surroundings on her own. She looked out one barred window, then the other. One gave her a view of a city, but it wasn't like the city she called home. The buildings were all made from stone or brick, with either slate or thatched roofs. The roads far below were paved with dirt and small rocks instead of the blacktop she was familiar with. She saw no sidewalks, but she realized those weren't necessary because she didn't see any cars either.

The other window gave her a view of a wild and unspoiled world that, except for a few farms here and there, seemed to be completely untouched by humans. Thick forests and open fields dotted the land, and tall purple-gray mountains capped with snow loomed high on the horizon.

It looked like a lovely place to explore . . . if only she could figure a way out of her cell.

She heard footsteps approaching and knew they couldn't belong to Anya. Carrie hadn't realized it until just that moment, but the girl hadn't made any sounds when she moved. It was like she'd been a figment of her imagination all along.

The door opened, and a single person stepped through. Carrie considered making a run for it, but the door swung shut and the lock clicked almost immediately.

The woman who entered the room looked like Anya, but she was older and taller. Despite making every effort at keeping her emotions hidden, Carrie couldn't help but give a small gasp of awe when she saw this newcomer. She was beautiful—no, more than beautiful. She looked *regal*, the way Carrie always used to imagine herself when she pretended to be a princess or a queen.

The woman didn't have a crown or scepter, but Carrie could tell she was somebody special. It was all in the way she carried herself, with a grace and poise that made it seem like some inner strength was just waiting to burst out of her. Her face was gentle and serene, framed by silky blonde hair. Her fine purple cloak and rust-colored dress completed the royal image.

"Sorceress," the woman said in a voice that commanded respect but which wasn't harsh. "If that is what you really are . . . I think we started off on the wrong foot."

"Kidnapping and locking me in a cell with some sort of ghost girl definitely sends an unpleasant message," Carrie responded.

The woman stood still and poised just a few feet inside the door, keeping her distance from Carrie, who returned to the bed where she had been "meditating" earlier. "Don't worry about Anya," she said. "She was just an aspect of myself." She waved her hand, and Anya appeared, then faded away again in a puff of smoke. "Just like many others." She waved her other hand, and the shadowy, clawed men appeared.

Carrie tensed despite the fact that she knew they, too, would disappear in a moment—which, of course, they did.

"They're parts of me, but they aren't the real me. My name is Melania."

"Melania . . . if Anya was just an illusion or something you created, why did she warn me about you?"

"When I brought you here, I needed you to think I was an enemy. I wanted to see how you would react. And you surprised me—you kept your head, and you kept your secrets as well. I respect you, Carrie, and I want to offer my aid. Maybe even my friendship."

"No offense, but my friends don't kidnap me."

Something strange flickered across the woman's face—was it shame? Melania sighed and sat on the bed on the opposite side of the room. "Please," she said in a less commanding tone of voice, "let me explain." Then she shook her head and sighed. "No . . . it will be easier to show you."

She clapped her hands, and the wall behind her vanished. The stone became shadow, then those shadows started to take shape. It was like Carrie was watching a movie, but with figures so real, she could reach out and touch them.

"The world I grew up on," Melania began, "was a world like yours, where magic exists but isn't something most people know about. My powers came to me when I was just a girl, and then . . ."

On the wall, Carrie saw somebody just a little younger than herself. That girl held out her hands, and green sparks flew from her fingertips. A bright smile quickly formed across the young face. Carrie found herself grinning—such simple, uncomplicated happiness. Was that what Sarah had felt when she first used her magic?

Rushing outside, the girl ran toward a crowd of people. The individuals, like the attackers who had captured her, seemed to be mostly uniform in appearance, lacking the unique features that made a person a person. When the girl created a sparkling bluebird with her spells, they didn't smile. Instead, they grabbed swords, clubs, and pitchforks. The girl fled, with the angry mob hot on her heels.

Carrie shrank back toward the opposite wall. Was that how people really reacted to magic? If so, would her lies about being a wizard get her into even more trouble than she was in now? As an enchantress herself, surely Melania wouldn't act like that . . . would she?

Back on the wall, the girl cried out for help. Two people came to her aid—her mother and father. Then fighting. Blood. Carrie looked away quickly as a sword slashed across the unprotected neck of the girl's father. When she looked back, she saw a headless body lying in a pool of blood.

The gruesome scene vanished.

"Your father gave his life to protect you," Carrie said. "I . . . well, I know people who have lost a parent. I'm sorry you went through that."

"Oh, it's not over," Melania said. "One of my parents died, but I lost both of them."

The images returned and grew darker. The girl's bright, shining magic became the stuff of shadows. She looked older, lines forming around her eyes and across her brow well before age should have put them there. The mother still wore a black mourning dress. When she looked at her daughter, there was no love in her eyes—only cold bitterness, as though she blamed the girl for the death of her husband.

The girl mouthed two words. No sound came out, but Carrie could read her lips: "I'm sorry."

The mother said nothing in response. She only raised her hand in anger.

Carrie turned away. When she looked back, the wall was just stone again. At the moment, she preferred to see a prison rather than Melania's past.

Melania folded her hands in her lap. Her face had gone pale, but her expression hadn't changed. Either she was no longer affected by the pain of the past or she'd learned to lock it away in a place where nobody else could see it.

"I thought my magic to be a simple miracle. I could create such lovely images. But people fear the unexplained, don't they? They'll do anything to get rid of it, and they don't care who they hurt. When a loved one dies, people look for somebody to blame . . . even if that somebody happens to be their own daughter."

Carrie remained silent. Melania had captured her and held her prisoner. She had all the control in the situation. Why, then, was she willing to make herself so vulnerable through this glimpse into her past?

"Ironically, they used magic to deal with me. One of their heroes found a magic sword that supposedly had the power to kill anybody it struck. But those people . . . they didn't really know what forces they were meddling with. The sword did defeat me, but it didn't kill me, just sent me to another world. It was a world of shadows, a place where I would be alone for years."

Melania shuddered at the memory but kept going nonetheless. "After that, I had nothing but my magic. I focused on my spells more and more each day. More than that, I focused on the world around me. Eventually, I bent the shadows to my will. I became the ruler of a world, but what good is that if you're the only one in the world? As the years went by, I learned how to take pieces of my own spirit and use them to create others. Anya . . . she was my only friend for a long time.

"Then, after years of isolation and loneliness, a door opened—not just a door, but the door to worlds that were better than mine. I came to this place called Greystone Valley, but it was a place in turmoil. The warlord who'd tried to bring order to this land had failed, and people were fighting all over. I knew I had the power to fix this wonderful land." She paused to glance out the window and beamed at what she saw. "In the space of a few months, I've fixed everything. Imagine a world where everybody is happy all the time, where there are no problems and no wars to fight.

"Now imagine three people with the power to ruin all that. They don't mean to—they think they're heroes. But when they found that the people of this land didn't need their help, their determination to be saviors blinded them to what was best for everyone. Then, two of them went to your world and tried to bring back a sorceress who could defeat me. I have reason to believe that the sorceress might be you. But that leaves an important question: If it is you, why are you hiding your abilities?"

Carrie looked into Melania's indigo-colored eyes and almost let the truth come tumbling past her lips. But just as it was about to slip off the tip of her tongue, she swallowed it and stuck with her story.

"I, um . . . What's a sorceress without her secrets?"

If the lie convinced Melania in any way, she didn't show it. However, her expression did soften, and her voice took on a gentler tone. "I'm sorry for the way I've treated you so far. All I knew was that I had to bring you to me before those others made contact with you. I didn't mean to be so rough. And then, with Anya . . . I was trying to figure out if you were the person I had to worry about. In many ways, I'm still trying to figure that out. There was a person with you when you were taken. Tell me . . . is this a case of mistaken identity?"

Carrie swallowed hard at the mention of Sarah. Friends or not, there were certain things she still owed her. "Not at all. She's . . . she's my apprentice, and I'd appreciate it if you didn't hurt her."

"You're young to have an apprentice, aren't you?"

"Not in my world." Carrie grinned. The more she spun these stories, the more she started to like it. Keeping them consistent while not tipping Melania off was an exciting challenge. "We go through a change at around my age. Once we've finished that change, we're considered full sorceresses and given the right to choose an apprentice if we want."

Melania stared into space, as though Carrie was invisible and she was studying the air behind her. "I think you might be lying to me."

Carrie felt a lump form in her throat and swallowed it down. "What does that mean for me?"

Her captor stood up. "I haven't decided yet. But I want you to know, whether you're an enchantress or not, I don't have any reason to fear you while you're my prisoner. I could erase your memory or imprison you deep underground where nobody will ever find you. But I don't want to. I'd like to come to an understanding with you. I'd like to take you on a walk through the Great City and show you how happy people are under my rule. Maybe you could even rule at my side. I want . . ." She sighed. "I want a friend. You seem like you could be that, but you need to stop lying to me."

Carrie curled her toes. "I'd love to stop lying, but I'm already telling you the truth."

A vein throbbed on Melania's forehead. "Very well," she said. "If you want to talk to me again, just knock on the door."

Without another word, the woman marched toward the exit and banged once. It swung open, and she stepped outside, slamming it behind her.

Carrie sighed. Outside, the sky bled orange and purple as the sun began to set. A whole evening gone. A whole night ahead of her with no escape in sight. Even if she got out of the cell, she was stuck in some distant world, maybe with no chance of ever seeing home again. Still, she had to try *something*.

She picked up the wand that Anya—or rather, Melania—had handed her. Poking around the room carefully, she finally found what she was hoping for: a little bit of cracked stone by the doorway. It wasn't much, but it was a place to start. Hoping that a magic wand was strong enough to handle this sort of use, Carrie started chipping away at the weak spot, hopefully digging her way to freedom.

Nine

As the companions finally began traveling again, Sarah marveled at the unspoiled land around her. Tall, lush trees looked like they touched the clouds and practically begged to be climbed. Massive gray boulders dotted the landscape, some with mysterious runes on them that not even her mom could decipher. Had it not been for the constant complaining of the wounded Dax, Sarah might have spent a few days exploring the vast untamed wilderness.

"The pain is terrible," the old warrior moaned, "but I suppose I had best get used to that. Every day I wake up with a new ache in my back or twinge in my leg. It's enough to ruin my normally sunny disposition."

From the sound of it, Dax would've been happier if they'd left the arrow in him. Sarah tried to tell herself that his griping was normal, but a simple look at him showed that he was in even more pain than he let on. He walked more gingerly than before, and the travelers had to stop every few hours to make sure his wound hadn't started bleeding again. Each time they did, Sarah felt smaller and smaller. Given time to heal, her mom assured her Dax would be fine. But there was almost certainly more fighting ahead, and Sarah couldn't help but feel a prickle of fear along her spine when she imagined the old warrior stumbling at an important point in a fight because of that wound she'd caused.

"So where to now?" Sarah asked, forcing herself to stay upbeat. "Were those beast-men part of Melania's army? Did we just win our first battle against her?"

"Even if they were, they probably wouldn't realize it," Kay said. "Remember when I said we couldn't beat her with swords? Somebody who can control the way people think doesn't need an army. If you asked most people when Melania became the ruler of Greystone Valley, they wouldn't be able to give you an answer. They'd just say she's always been there."

"If she took over without a fight and nobody seems to mind, what's the problem? Is she some kind of tyrant or something?"

"Sort of. You'll see when we get to the Great City."

"Also, I don't think it can be pointed out enough that her minions did kidnap your friend," Dax added.

"Good point." Sarah straightened her posture and put on a determined look. "So, where are we going?"

"Underground. From there, Keeley knows the way!" The dragon did a loop-de-loop in the air. "She knows all the twists and turns in the tunnels down below."

"Yes," Dax replied, "but need I remind you that the creatures who live in those tunnels have a dim view of dragons at best, even if those dragons happen to be tiny and helpful?"

"Oh, Dax, of course Keeley remembers that! How could she forget how they chased her and tried to chop her with their axes? But Keeley is far too fast for them, so it's really just a game! And if they do get too close, she can always hide under Kay's hat like she did before."

"Let's keep the games to a minimum, especially when they involve deadly weapons." Dax poked his crudely bandaged wound and winced. "We've had enough accidents already."

"Why do we need to go underground?" Sarah asked.

"Believe me, if there was a better way to approach without being seen, we would take it," Dax responded. "I hate those tunnels—they're so dank and dreary. The moisture and cold air will almost certainly make my rheumatism act up. But Castle Greystone is surrounded by trackless foothills and thick forests. The southern pass is our best hope of getting to the Great City. The caverns are dark and deep, but they'll bring us right beneath the city, although I'm sure we'll all perish before we're through."

"So, what will we be facing down there?" Sarah's mom asked. "Dragons? Trolls?"

"Worse," Dax said. "Dwarves."

"Dwarves?" Sarah asked. "Like short people?"

"Short, hairless people that live in the deepest caverns and . . . ugh . . . sing sometimes."

"They don't sound that bad."

Dax scanned the horizon and took the lead as they got going. "Sometimes," he moaned, "it seems like everybody else is speaking in a foreign language."

The journey to the pass took most of the rest of the day, giving Sarah and her mom a chance to re-acquaint themselves with the valley. Every ridge and hill seemed familiar, even if they hadn't been there before. The higher up they got in the foothills, the more they could see. Sarah pointed out to her mom the small village where she'd first come to this world, convinced that she was just dreaming rather than the victim of yet another botched spell from Kay. Excited by the rekindling of her own memories, her mom seemed to forget that she was still angry at Sarah for her foolishness against the beast-men, instead listening with delight as her daughter regaled her with tales of meeting dragons and fighting trolls.

When Sarah described her meeting with the tiny winged fey, she stopped suddenly and couldn't continue until she asked her mom an important question.

"When the faeries put you to sleep back there, some . . . thing named Sabrina showed up. She said she was your grandmother or great-grandmother. Is that true?"

"Sabrina . . ." Her mom said the name slowly, as though uttering it too quickly might summon her. "Well, she's not exactly my grand-mother, but she is an ancestor. You and I, we're part of this valley but not part of it. We're not natives, because we were raised elsewhere. But we belong here because we're descended from Sabrina. Her magic runs through our veins."

"She said she was the one who helped Melania change everybody's memories. Do you think she might be able to undo that spell?"

"I'm sure she could, sweetie, but there would be a price . . . one we shouldn't pay unless we have no other options."

"She said she wanted to keep you in the valley for years."

"That sounds like her. She's very old and doesn't realize how long a year is to us. She means well, but she doesn't know what mortal life is anymore."

"Do you think she'll try to kidnap one of us again?"

"I don't know. She's too unpredictable for me to reasonably guess. When I was younger, sometimes she would let me come and go without ever appearing. Other times, she tried to make sure I never left. She's not evil, really, but I wouldn't suggest calling on her unless we don't have any other options."

"I've heard of Sabrina before," interjected Kay, who had been lis-tening to their conversation with growing interest. "Supposedly, she was the wife of the great wizard who created this valley. She taught him most of what he knew. But shortly after the valley was formed, she met Pan, the leader of the fey. They fell in love, and she left the wizard. According to legend, he cursed her so when she died, her spirit didn't go on to the afterlife."

"Well, that would explain why she had to make herself a body out of roots and branches, then," Sarah said.

Kay nodded. "Sure . . . somebody like her wouldn't let a little thing like dying of old age stop her from talking to her descendants. The wizard eventually became stronger than her, but she knew some incredibly powerful magic on her own. It was with her help that the wizard wrote my spellbook, which contained all the magic anybody has ever known."

"Your spellbook . . ." Sarah suddenly realized that, unlike her and her mom, Kay was running around without a book to draw his spells from. "Where is your spellbook anyway?"

"Destroyed, of course." Kay said the words almost cheerfully. "The last time we were both at Castle Greystone, it got damaged. Uh, catastrophically so."

"Then how are you able to remember so many spells without it?"

"Remember?"

"Yes, silly! To cast a spell, you need to say the right words, syllable-for-syllable. If I didn't take the time to study up on all those spells once in a while, I'd never be able to keep them all straight."

"Well, unlike you, I could never read a spellbook very well anyway. Too many weird symbols in the place of honest-to-goodness words. After you went home the last time, I had to find my way back to Keeley and Dax. So I, uh . . . winged it."

"You winged it?"

"Yeah . . . I just imagined what I wanted my magic to do, then I said the words that seemed right for the situation. It works out pretty well for me—most of the time, that is."

Stunned, Sarah lagged behind as Kay kept following Dax. She turned to her mom with a baffled expression on her face. "Mom? Is that even possible?"

Sarah's mom shrugged. "I know two things, sweetie. First, there's something very special about your friend that I don't think even he realizes just yet. Second, I think we know now why his spells tend to backfire."

By sunset, they reached a gaping tunnel that sloped sharply downward a few dozen feet inside. They decided at this point to rest for the night—or rather, Dax's wound decided for them. As soon as they got a few feet into the cave, the old warrior dropped in a heap and had trouble getting up again. Sarah's mom changed his bandages and set up a watch schedule that had each of the four other companions taking a short shift during the night.

After that, it was just a matter of getting to the meager fare Kay and Dax had brought along for food. Dax's pack had some basic supplies, but even Sarah's mom could only do so much with nuts, dried strips of venison, and a jar of porridge, especially when she only had a campfire to work with. The supplies did contain a small amount of honey, but her mom didn't want to use too much of that so they would still have some later on. Keeley did some quick foraging and made several trips back with berries in her claws—as well as a few bugs and one small newt that were definitely appetizing only to the dragon.

Sarah munched on the venison and sweetened porridge, finding it nourishing but not exactly enjoyable. She decided that the next time she came to Greystone Valley, she would make sure to bring a thermos full of her mom's chicken and dumplings. And maybe a large pizza. And . . . well, the list of things she would rather be eating went on and on.

Her mom took the first watch, and nobody complained. Miles of walking through rough terrain had taken a lot out of everybody, and they all wanted some rest. Keeley twitched and talked in her sleep, and Kay snored so loudly that Sarah was afraid he'd wake up every creature in the mountains. Neither of them was enough to keep her from a nap of her own, though. A few minutes after she closed her eyes, she fell into a dreamless slumber.

She woke up a few hours before dawn. Keeley was nibbling at her toes, letting her know it was her turn at watch. She slipped on her shoes and moved so she was sitting cross-legged at the mouth of the cave a few feet away from Dax.

A crescent moon hung over the valley, casting a very pale silver glow over the surrounding hills. The more Sarah watched, the more she thought she saw figures in the distance. Shadows on the top of the hill seemed to move in some sort of secret dance that nobody else in the area knew about. Some of them skulked about, while others frolicked. They seemed to have a rhythm to them, but Sarah couldn't hear whatever music they were moving to.

"You're watching the shadows, of course. It must be fey playing in the night. They're not all as tiny as bugs. Some are as big as giants, though no less graceful."

The sound of Dax's voice made Sarah jump, because she could have sworn that he'd been sound asleep just a few seconds ago.

"Forgive me," the old warrior said. "Your mother did a wonderful job dressing the wound, but it still aches. And when you're as old as I am, all it takes is one or two things out of place to keep you from getting a sound sleep."

"I would have thought the hard ground would be enough to keep you awake, then," Sarah responded.

"Hard ground? Dear me, no. When you travel as much as Kay, Keeley, and I have, you get used to sleeping on roots, stones, and all manner of other rough terrain. By now, I think a comfortable feather bed would keep me from getting a sound sleep. I simply wouldn't know what to do with it."

"Dax, can I change the subject for a minute?"

"By all means, please do. I know my ramblings can get boring. That's why I don't talk to myself, you know. I wouldn't be able to tolerate the company."

"You know my mother."

"Passingly. We had an adventure or two together in the valley many years ago."

"Why didn't you tell me you knew her? I didn't find out she had been to this world until after I had already gone home."

"Would it have made you feel better if you had known?"

"Yes! I mean, I think it would have. At the very least, it would have explained why I had such a knack for magic. I would have known I was the daughter of the Emerald Enchantress!"

Dax tapped the side of his head. "Then I'm sorry, and I have to blame my puny brain. Maybe I noticed a family resemblance—you certainly do look like your mother, after all—but I don't think I ever assumed it was anything but wishful thinking on my part. And, of course, there's the other thing . . ."

"What other thing?"

"A lost girl in a strange valley who was just learning how to cast spells for the first time . . . I didn't want to add even more insanity on top of that for you. If I had told you that you were possibly the daughter of a legendary sorceress—possibly, mind you, because I didn't know for sure—that would have added even more pressure on top of what you were already going through." Dax rolled over so his back was to Sarah. "Trust me, I know it's hard enough to just live your life without putting yourself into somebody else's shadow all the time. I'm the thirteenth son of a thirteenth son. Imagine somebody that unlucky trying to live up to his heroic cousin, the seventh son of a seventh son."

"Is that why you're happier in Greystone Valley than in your home world?"

"Happy? Who is ever happy? Good night, my dear."

Within a few minutes, Dax's breathing returned to the deep, rhythmic cycle of sleep. Sarah scooted over toward him. Then she leaned over and kissed him gently on the cheek. "Good night, Dax. Have sweet dreams. At least something about you deserves to be pleasant."

Ten

s she watched the dawn, Sarah wondered if her mom had given her the last shift of the night as a gift. The sky shone purple and orange, as though some invisible creature was painting the heavens, and the colors only got more vibrant from there.

The figures that had danced so gracefully through the mountains swayed in the morning light, shifting in color as the sun cast orange-yellow rays over the mountains that made them look like they were made of gold.

She turned to wake the others and show them the beautiful sunrise, but her pleasant mood evaporated when she noticed that the five companions weren't alone. A small gray-skinned creature had somehow managed to sneak into the area despite her careful watch. A little bit taller than waist height to Sarah, the little thing smelled like greasy fish and wore clothes that looked like they were probably fashioned out of moldy potato sacks. At the moment, the creature seemed content to repeatedly thrust a blackened stick into the red embers of their fire, but Sarah wasn't about to give it a chance to do anything else.

The rest of the companions awoke to the shout of Sarah's spell as a wave of her wand sent the tiny monster hurtling into a wall. Much to her surprise, the thing didn't seem to be hurt by the impact or panicked by the superior numbers that now faced it. Instead, it picked itself up, hopped from foot to foot, and clapped its hands.

"Good trick! Good trick!" From its pockets, it pulled two egg-like objects. "My turn now!"

The thing threw the small objects, which shattered on the ground at Sarah's feet. A burst of brownish-yellow vapor came from them, and Sarah nearly retched as everything started smelling like rotten eggs. It was the type of stink that seemed to have a physical presence—Sarah was sure it would take weeks to wash the odor out of her clothes and hair.

Then she realized that the horrible smell was the least of her problems. The smoke left a thick dust that clung to her nose, mouth, and eyes. In a split second, the entire world became covered in a yellow haze. Sarah found herself gasping for air, but this only made the problem worse. The deeper she breathed, the more smoke she took in. In a moment, she was on her knees coughing and sputtering and unsure if it would be better for her to continue to struggle for air or just try to hold her already limited breath.

The rest of the companions, caught off guard and barely awake, were in the same terrible situation. Sarah's ears were greeted by gasping and choking sounds from the others in the cavern. Then, probably the most ominous sound of all—sneezing from Keeley.

Barely able to see anything, Sarah got to her feet and grabbed the nearest person she could get hold of. She thought it would be Dax, but he must have either been slow to get up or quick to move toward the potential threat. She fell down, dragging the slender figure underneath her and pinning him to the ground. It was Kay, who was as miserable and breathless as she was.

Keeley's coughing and sputtering quickly gave way to a roar of flame as the dragon started sneezing uncontrollably. In the blinding haze around them, it would be impossible to control where those fireballs went. Sarah only hoped that the little dragon was as lucky as she was cute.

The fire helped burn some of the haze away, but it only made the stench worse. Now, it was like somebody had lit a skunk on fire.

As visibility started to return in the cave, Sarah saw that Keeley had indeed been both careful and lucky. After the first couple of fireballs, she had clapped her front claws over her mouth and held her breath. Unfortunately, that meant even less air for her tiny lungs. As a result, she was the first to drop unconscious.

In the confusion, Sarah had actually moved past Dax, who was fumbling for his swords but already too weak from lack of air to stand. Her mom waved her wand wildly and tried to recite the words to a spell but was left as nothing more than a choking and gasping mess. Underneath the layer of dust the smoke cloud had caused, Kay's face was turning blue. Sarah guessed she probably looked just as bad.

Spots formed in front of Sarah's eyes as she looked at the cause of all the chaos. The little gray man stood with his back pressed against the cavern wall, just outside the area of the smoke.

"What fun! What fun!" he chuckled with glee.

Sarah pushed herself off Kay and staggered forward, intent on showing him the sort of "fun" he seemed to crave. She found it hard to make good on her intentions, though. Her legs felt like lead, and the lack of air was getting to her.

The cackling of the little man was soon joined by other voices, moving up from deeper in the tunnel. More small feet rushed toward the companions. Unlike the first one, they didn't seem concerned with stealth, doubtless realizing their prey couldn't even breathe, let alone defend themselves.

"Look! Look! New playmates!" the first creature shouted.

Sarah was the lucky one. Having breathed in more of the smoke than the others, she finally succumbed to her lack of air and collapsed, colors swirling in her vision as her mind rushed toward blackness. Before she passed out entirely, she heard pained sounds from her companions. Unlike Sarah and Keeley, they hadn't been lucky enough to simply pass out. Instead, the swarm of little men rushed them, beating them with clubs and stones until they joined Sarah in unconsciousness.

The fact that Sarah could breathe when she woke up again surprised her. She took deep gasps of air, thankful that she had indeed woken up and not been left to die on the floor of the cavern. The air felt stale and old as it came into her lungs, but she didn't care.

The rest of her companions woke up in a similar way. She heard them gasp deeply and then groan in pain as the bruises they'd suffered washed over their newly conscious bodies. Her hands were tied behind her with cords that had been drawn tight enough to hurt her wrists. Her feet were free, but the cackles of many little monsters around her told her it would be best to stay down until she and her friends could figure a way out of . . . wherever they were.

They certainly weren't at the cave opening anymore, where Sarah now silently cursed herself for watching the sunrise rather than paying more attention to the things that might be coming out of the ground. She didn't know where they were, except that the sun didn't shine there. In fact, there was no light at all except for a circle of fire which ran a ring around the five companions, giving them only about a yard to move even if they were able to get to their feet. Dozens of small shadows danced and giggled beyond the fire, amused by the peril the companions now found themselves in.

"They wake! And if they move too much, they bake!"

"Goody goody! More games to play!"

"Do you think Kytar will let me wear the tall one's hat?"

Sarah gritted her teeth and tuned out the cackles, instead focusing on the well-being of her companions. The four humans had been pressed together in a circle, each bound hand and foot like Sarah. Keeley lay at Sarah's feet, hog-tied and with a ball of twine around her snout. The little dragon flapped her wings furiously, but without her legs to maneuver herself, all she managed to do was spin herself in a circle on the floor.

Kay had awoken at Sarah's left, her mom at her right. Behind her, she felt what could only be Dax's back pressed against her own. Injured before the ambush had begun, the old warrior seemed to spend all his energy just trying to breathe. He didn't even have the strength to complain about all the new aches and pains he'd just acquired.

"I'm sorry," Sarah said. "I didn't notice we were being ambushed until it was too late."

"Don't be sorry," Kay responded. "Gremlins can be all but invisible when they want to be. You probably wouldn't have seen him even if you'd been looking right at him."

"It wasn't . . . really an ambush," Dax groaned sluggishly. "To them, this is all a game. A very cruel game where somebody will probably get killed. And people wonder why I don't like to think about 'fun' in this valley."

"Are you okay, Dax?" Sarah asked. Then, thinking about her question a bit more, she added, "I mean . . . relatively speaking?"

"For somebody who has been shot, suffocated, and bludgeoned? No, not really. I think my rheumatism is acting up again."

"Gremlins," Sarah's mom said. "I think I ran into them once or twice, long ago."

"Thankfully, not while I was with you," Dax said. "When it comes to obnoxious tricksters, you've basically got two varieties. There are the fey, who think it's fun to be annoying but whose games are usually harmless. They'll steal your underwear or cast a spell that will make your nose grow, but unless they think you're a threat, you don't have to worry about them being anything more than obnoxious. Gremlins like pranks, too, but . . ." He quieted down, letting the chanting and jeering of the little monstrosities fill the area. "Us nearly choking to death and then getting our skulls clubbed in is all good fun to them."

"So we're helpless . . . and they're going to have more 'fun,'" Sarah said gloomily.

"Almost certainly," Dax responded. "I didn't want to say anything for fear of bringing your mood down, but we're all doomed."

Sarah strained at her bonds, only to find that the rope seemed to be as strong as steel. Yet despite that, they seemed to have some give to them. The gremlins must have been careless in tying her up . . . a mistake she looked forward to making them regret.

In another second, Sarah realized that it wasn't a mistake on the part of the gremlins, but rather help from the very person who had made the situation seem the most hopeless. Even as he droned on about his aches and pains, Dax's fingers had been working at the knots around Sarah's wrists. The progress was clumsy and slow, but it was progress nonetheless.

Inwardly, Sarah smiled. She almost returned the favor and tried to get Dax loose but instead held as still as possible so he could more effectively free her. If one of them was going to break loose, better somebody who could drive her enemies off with magic than a lone warrior who had already experienced more than his fair share of injuries.

The shouts and jeers died away eventually, giving way to a long silence, during which time the crackle of the flames around them was the only sound. Sarah guessed that some sort of chemical not unlike the strange suffocating powder was causing the fire. At least that's what it smelled like. It definitely wasn't wood, and it made her eyes water as though somebody had poured gasoline on a pile of old socks.

"Does anything involving these creatures not smell awful?" Sarah whispered.

"Silence!" said a man in a high, shrill voice. "You shall insult neither the people of the depths nor their aroma!"

"Well, it's not really an insult, is it?" asked another man's voice, this one sounding calmer and more reasonable. "It's really more of an observation."

The gremlins chuckled and whispered before hushing themselves up to hear the first voice's reaction.

"Etten, do you really need to embarrass me like this every time we bring people down here?"

"Only if you're going to embarrass me by pretending that we're some sort of mysterious dark lords. Why not just be forthright about it?"

"Because we have an army of gremlins at our disposal! What else are we supposed to do?"

"Um . . . excuse me?" Sarah called. "Can we just get on with this?"

"See? There's somebody with the common courtesy to sit there and be threatened."

"Oh, shut up. She's only saying that because those ropes are probably cutting off the blood flow to her brain."

The higher-pitched voice took a deep breath before starting again, as if hoping that the companions would forget the awkward opening. "Extinguish the flames!"

With a cackle and a sneer, the gremlins closest to the fire threw dirt on it. Smoke filled the inky blackness, leaving all the companions completely blinded. All the while, though, Dax never stopped trying to untie the ropes around Sarah's wrists.

Footsteps approached in the darkness, and then the sound of a stick striking stone echoed through the chamber. In immediate response, several of the gremlins lit torches, illuminating a new cavern, larger and deeper than the one the companions had been in before.

Sarah remembered wanting to face an army of beast-men before. Now, if she got free in time, she would probably wind up facing a throng of gremlins. Dozens of the grimy creatures encircled them, lining up as far back as Sarah could see. Some of them had gray skin like the one that had attacked them in the first place, others looked warty and green, and still more had craggy faces that seemed to blend in naturally with the gray and white granite that dominated most of the cavern.

The two people who had been speaking didn't look like gremlins at all. They stood in front of Sarah and Keeley, and they looked like very short humans . . . or rather, humans who might once have been normally proportioned but who had somehow been squashed downward. They stood barely over four feet in height and seemed almost as wide as they were tall. Despite their girth, they both seemed muscular, although the more sensible one had a pot belly in addition to his brawny arms. Neither of them had any sort of hair on their heads, save for very bushy eyebrows. The shrill-voiced one had chalky-colored skin and had a slender blade at his side in a gold-lined scabbard. The other one wielded only a staff and had glossy brown skin like polished cedar.

"Do you see how helpless you are now?" the one with the sword said to Sarah. "Our gremlins listen to us because we provide them with these lovely diversions. If you aren't careful, we might leave and let them have their fun."

"Kytar," the one who was apparently named Etten said, "let's just get to the point."

"What do you want?" Sarah asked.

"It's not a matter of what we want," Kytar started. "It's—"

"Yes, it is," Etten interrupted.

"What?"

"It *is* a matter of what we want. That's the whole point."

Sarah glanced at Kay. The expression on his face told him that he was reasonably sure he was still unconscious and dreaming this whole situation.

"Fine," the increasingly ill-tempered Kytar said. "You explain it."

"I will," Etten responded. Leaning in close to the companions, he said loudly and clearly, "We're robbing you."

"Well, you're out of luck there," Sarah's mom said. "We're traveling lightly—only the supplies we absolutely need and the clothes on our backs."

"We know that now," Kytar said. "We had plenty of time to look through your belongings after we captured you."

"To be honest," Etten said in a hushed tone, "you can blame the gremlins. We've asked them to focus on travelers who look wealthy, but they just can't help themselves. But now you're here, and we need to offer our minions something that can amuse them. I'm afraid that books, sticks, and a few scraps of dried meat just won't do."

"Of course, there's always the ransom option," Kytar said. "Melania did ask us to keep an eye out for spellcasters, and there are at least three of them in this group."

"Do you really think our . . . friends . . . have the patience to wait until we deliver them to Melania and hope she'll pay us a proper reward?" Etten asked.

Kytar turned slowly and surveyed the horde of gremlins around him. Many of them were starting to fidget and grumble with impatience. A few were fingering knives. "No," he admitted. "Probably not."

Sarah felt one of the knots around her wrist come loose. She nudged Kay hard, hoping that he would get the unspoken message that they needed to keep their captors talking for just a little longer.

"Wait a minute," Kay said. "You're dwarves! Your people protect the mountains—they don't work with gremlins and rob travelers."

At Kay's objection, Kytar got red in the face and stamped his foot. "Why do you humans always assume all dwarves are alike? If I used you lot as a judge of what all humans were like, I'd have to assume that half of you were nitwit children, a quarter of you were old, doddering twits, and only one in four of you had the sense to stay quiet!"

"Look at it this way," Etten said in a more reasonable voice. "Dwarves traditionally protect the riches of the earth. We just happen to be of the mind that we should gather those riches that have been mined—gold, gems, and the like—and bring them back where they belong. Happily, we live in the place we bring them back to."

"And you should be grateful we're different from the dwarves you know, boy!" Kytar screeched. "Otherwise, your pet dragon would be gremlin food right now!"

Keeley growled and struggled against her bonds more fiercely, furious at being referred to as somebody's pet.

"Don't worry, Keeley," Sarah whispered. "They'll eat their words."

The last of the bonds around her wrist slipped free. Sarah pushed her hands against the stone floor and used the force to propel her onto her feet.

"Stay back!" Kytar hollered, waving his sword fearfully. "Stay back!"

She came up, planning to send a burst of lightning through the chamber but stopped short of casting the spell when she realized she'd made a mistake—the same kind of foolish mistake she'd made against the beast-men. She'd focused too much on the enemies she could see, ignoring the ones at her back.

Sure enough, a glance over her shoulder saw that at least ten gremlins stood grinning behind her, eager to see what this new development offered. Two of them already had knives out, and one of them held a tiny bow with an arrow already nocked in it. The fear of one of those weapons striking Dax or another one of her companions again stopped her cold.

It took only a second for Sarah to come to a decision.

"I surrender," Sarah said, putting up her hands.

Her mom groaned. "Sarah," she said, "this is absolutely the worst possible time you could have started listening to me."

Eleven

"**W**ell," Kytar cackled. "That must be the shortest escape attempt in history!"

Both the dwarves and the gremlins laughed loudly. Sarah felt her face flush as she realized her mistake. She should have been more patient, picked her spot instead of jumping up as soon as she could. She promised herself she would find a way to fix her mistake and quickly came up with what she could loosely call a plan.

"You didn't let me finish my sentence," she said as the laughter died down. "I meant to say, I surrender . . . if you can beat me in a duel."

Kytar's eyes bulged and he pointed his sword threateningly at Sarah's chest. "What?"

Sarah turned toward her audience. "You want fun and games, right?"

The throng of gremlins shouted, cheered, and giggled in agreement.

"There's no reason to put everyone at risk," Sarah said. "Give me a sword. You and I can duel, and that will satisfy the gremlins. If you win, my friends will still be at your mercy. If I win, you let us go and show us the way back to the surface."

"You're surrounded and outnumbered. Why should I listen to you?"

Sarah pointed her hand toward Kytar's face. The tips of her fingers glowed slightly as a spell etched itself in her mind and magical energy prepared to explode out of her. "Because while I wouldn't be able to escape completely, I could still fry you before I went down."

Kytar wrinkled his nose as if he was trying to close his nostrils. Etten defused the situation with a booming laugh.

"What a wonderful solution! Come on, Kytar, you're not afraid of losing a duel to a child, are you?"

"A child sorceress!" the visibly nervous dwarf shrieked. "I know better than to cross swords with magic!"

"No spells," Sarah said. "I promise. My friend Dax had two swords. Give me the smaller one." She cast her eyes behind her toward the gremlin she'd seen with a bow. "That one can keep its bow pointed at me. If I don't fight fairly, he can shoot me."

"Hm . . . very well," Kytar said. He nodded to Etten, who left for a moment to retrieve the sword for Sarah.

"Sarah," her mom whispered. "Have you ever even used a sword?"

"I've been to this valley before, remember?"

"That doesn't even come close to answering my question." She glanced at Kay, who shrugged and shook his head.

"Stop!" her mom said. "Let me fight in her place!"

"No," Kytar said with a snort. "She asked first."

"You coward!" Her mom strained against the ropes, and for a moment, Sarah was certain she would break right out of them. "You'd dare fight a child?"

Etten answered the question, having returned with the blade. "Madam, by now, it should be obvious that fighting a child is one of the only things we *would* dare to do."

Sarah took the sword confidently and tested its weight. "It's okay, Mom. How hard can it be?"

"Extremely hard if you don't position your feet right," Dax said, craning his neck around to see Sarah's positioning. "Your back foot needs to be perpendicular to your front."

Sarah looked at her feet in confusion. "Perpendicular? Is that when they're side by side?"

Dax groaned. "Far be it from me to call something hopeless, but . . ."

"Enough talk!" Kytar waved the bow-wielding gremlin forward. Grinning stupidly, the creature drew back the bowstring and pointed the weapon at Sarah.

"Wait," the dwarf said. He looked sharply into Sarah's eyes as if trying to figure out why the girl seemed so confident despite the peril she was in. "Change of rules. If she cheats, shoot that one."

He pointed at Kay. The gremlin, satisfied with the chance of shooting anyone, obediently shifted his aim.

"Still want to play?" the dwarf asked with a grin.

"Don't worry, Sarah!" Kay said bravely. "I have—"

"Let's go," Sarah said without a moment of hesitation.

"Oh," a crestfallen Kay mumbled.

Kytar took a graceful dueling stance that made the heavy-set dwarf seem like a dancer. Sarah made sure to stand a good distance away to start so the dwarf would have to move toward her to strike her with a lunge. She tried to mimic the fighting stance she'd seen Dax take but found it uncomfortable. Instead, she stood flat-footed, facing the dwarf straight on and holding her sword with both hands.

The rest of the companions closed their eyes in dread . . . all except for Kay, who stared gravely at the arrow pointed at him.

"Ready?" Etten called. "And . . . go!"

As soon as the battle began, Sarah threw her sword at Kytar's face.

The attack was clumsy, but it was fast and unexpected enough that the dwarf had no defense. The sword turned in the air so the blade missed him, but the hilt smashed against his nose hard enough to draw blood.

"D'ow!" Kytar shouted, dropping his sword in surprise. "By doze! She broke by dose!"

While her foe was still recovering from the shock, Sarah leapt upon him. Her fighting was far from graceful or honorable, but it was effective. Using her size to her advantage, she grappled with Kytar, kicking him in the shins and raking her nails wherever she could. He retaliated with some punches to her midsection which Sarah knew would hurt later, but her unfettered fury allowed her to ignore the pain for now.

The gremlins cackled and howled in delight. Some of them even started fighting amongst themselves, mimicking Sarah's vicious attacks and Kytar's undignified howling defense. Even the gremlin with the bow seemed more interested in the battle than where he was pointing his weapon.

"Stop! Stop! This isn't—agh!" Any coherent words that Kytar had to offer in his defense disappeared when Sarah managed to grab hold of his bushy eyebrows and started pulling with all her might.

"Do you yield?" Sarah kept one hand on one of Kytar's eyebrows and twisted his ear viciously with the other.

"Yes! Yes! I yield! I yield!"

Sarah let go of her opponent, who now had scratch marks all along his bald head, blood dripping from his cheeks, and even less hair than before. Sarah herself had trouble standing straight now that she felt the aches and pains left from Kytar's blows. But she wasn't nearly as bad off—winning had a way of taking the edge off the pain.

"Well, now," she said. "If I were to use you as a judge of what all dwarves were like, I would think that none of them could beat a thirteen-year-old girl."

Etten took a few moments to shout and wave the gremlins to silence while Kytar brushed himself off, sheathed his sword, and tried to recover his pride. Sarah watched him warily, but the dwarf didn't make a move against either her or her companions. In fact, he waved the gremlin with the bow away, guaranteeing Kay's safety.

"You certainly shouldn't think that all dwarves would fall to those same tactics, my dear," Etten said. "In fact, I'm pretty sure that my partner here would do much better if you gave him a rematch."

"You can bet on that!" Kytar yelled, his voice even shriller than before. "You cheated! I should have the gremlins attack right now!"

"Oh, Kytar," Etten said. "Don't bluster. It doesn't suit you. They have nothing of value, and look at our friends." He gestured toward the cackling and shrieking gremlins. "Are they not entertained? It's time to keep our word for a change."

"Fine," Kytar grumbled. "Get them out of my sight and out of my life!"

"I think it's best if I lead you lot out of here," Etten said. "Kytar might be more likely to bring you to a troll's den out of spite."

Etten drew a knife from his belt and cut the companions' ropes. As soon as her mom was free, she leapt to her feet and threw her arms around Sarah. The hug didn't quite keep her from breathing, but combined with her bruises from the fight, it felt like her bones might turn to jelly.

"You are going to give me a heart attack, young lady. We are going to have a long talk about that particularly stupid idea of yours."

"It wasn't a stupid idea, Mom," Sarah retorted. "I knew I could win."

"That's not an excuse. If you had planned better, you wouldn't have had to fight at all. Though I do have to admit," she said, giving Sarah one more hug, "Kytar obviously doesn't have much experience. Otherwise, he would have known better than to pick a fight with an angry teenager."

Twelve

Carrie didn't mind calling herself a damsel, but being in distress was something she wanted no part of. Unfortunately, it didn't seem like she had much of a choice.

Her fingers were raw and a little bloody from her work, but at least she'd managed to chip away a little bit of the stone around the lower corner of her cell door. Based on how she had seen the door open when Melania had exited, she had a guess about where the hinge might be, and she guessed that it would be exposed soon if she kept working.

It had taken her an entire day to get to this point, although there had been plenty of delays. Every time she thought she heard footsteps or voices coming near the door, she hastily dashed back to bed, tucked the wand under her pillow, and pretended to be asleep.

Most times, it had been nothing. Once, the door opened and then closed immediately. Through one half-opened eye, she saw Melania walk quietly into the room and place a tray down on the table. Then her captor turned and stared directly at Carrie for a long, uncomfortable moment. She didn't move any closer, and she didn't say anything—she just looked with a frown on her face and her thin eyebrows furrowed. Then she left, closing the door quickly behind her.

After this visit, Carrie made sure to take the small collection of dirt and gravel her work had produced and drop it out her cell window so Melania wouldn't have a chance to notice her escape attempt. Then she felt a grumble in her stomach and decided to inspect the food.

The covered silver dish on the tray held two plates of food—dinner and breakfast, she assumed. The dinner was a well-seasoned cut of meat, some fresh green vegetables, and an apple. She took a cautious bite of the meat. She recognized it as duck, which she'd only had once before. She had eaten it with her family on a vacation years ago and thought it to be terribly greasy. This time, though, it seemed to have been prepared to perfection.

The breakfast caught Carrie by surprise. Rather than something like cereal, oatmeal, or pancakes, Melania had provided her with some sort of dried fish, a large loaf of bread, and a wedge of yellow cheese.

The tray also came with two large wooden cups. One was water and the other . . . was that wine? She took an experimental sip and was greeted with a taste that was both sweet and bitter at the same time. Grinning and figuring that this was a rare chance to do something her parents would never allow, she took a long swig of it. No sooner had the liquid hit the back of her throat than she gagged. She coughed most of it up, leaving a red stain on the circular rug under the table. Her eyes watered, and her nose burned. She put the cup back and decided to leave it alone.

Maybe wine wasn't her thing after all.

Despite her hunger, Carrie decided to return to her project before dinner. Surveying her handiwork, she sighed with disappointment. She'd broken away all the rock she could and formed a small opening that still didn't quite give her access to the hinge on the other side of the door. If she could figure out some way to get through, she could undo the hinge and make the door unstable enough to get loose. Then . . . well, who knew what she would do then?

With the sunlight fading, she decided to call it a night. She ate her dinner in silence, drank some of the water, and then looked at the tin chamber pot at the far end of the room. Maybe that would be strong enough to use as a tool, but she needed it for something else right now, and she certainly didn't want to move it after she was done.

Usually, Carrie took a nice, hot shower and listened to some music while her hair dried before bed. She didn't think she'd be able to sleep without these important parts of her routine, but the day's exertions had tired her out more than she'd expected. Her head hit the pillow, and she was out in a matter of minutes.

Her dreams started out as a confusing swirl of shadows, with voices speaking in strange languages and faces she couldn't see. Eventually, those noises and shapes formed into something she could understand.

Sounds of a fight emerged from outside. Steel clanged against steel as swords crossed in a frenzy. Then came a banging on the door. Somebody was breaking in.

Carrie sat bolt upright in her bed as the door split down the middle from one strong blow. She saw somebody's hand emerge from between the crack, pushing one side of the broken wood away. Then her rescuing hero stepped inside, making his identity known.

It was Kay—not the boy she remembered from school who'd stood by meekly while Sarah threw a fist at him, but a stronger, more muscular Kay who wore a suit of silver armor and wielded a sword. Carrie felt a nervous excitement build inside her body as she watched her hero walk toward her. His armor clanked loudly as he approached. He sheathed his blade, then leaned in close enough to kiss her.

Carrie felt a flutter in her chest as she tried to decide whether she would return the incoming kiss or not. Then Kay spoke softly.

"Kippers."

"What?" she asked in confusion.

"They're called kippers," he said.

Carrie opened her eyes, and her fanciful dream came to a decidedly unromantic ending.

"Oh," she said in disappointment.

Sunrise crept in through the windows of her prison. She looked at the fish that would serve as her breakfast.

Kippers. She remembered them now from one time when her mom had wanted to try a new recipe. The majority of her family didn't like them. She didn't mind their salty taste, but she still wished they'd stayed out of her dreams.

Despite being upset at her rescue being just a dream, she did eat the kippers and drink down the rest of the water. She needed to keep her strength up, after all. The dream had certainly been nice, but she knew for certain that if anybody was going to rescue her, it wasn't going to be Kay—or anybody else from her world, for that matter.

She decided to try a new tactic, wedging the now-empty serving tray between the door and the stone wall at the point where she had weakened the wall. She pushed the wand into the crack too and strained with all her might, trying to use the tools as levers to widen the space. The wand cracked, and the tray bent, but she did feel a slight shift in the door. It was barely anything, but she had slender enough hands that she could slip two fingers in.

Trembling from the exertion, she fumbled around for a few minutes before finally finding the thing she was looking for: the metal hinge on the other side of the door. Biting her lip to help her keep her concentration, she felt the bottom part of the hinge's pin. She twisted and pulled until she finally got the satisfying reward of a pinging noise as metal hit the floor. Carrie collapsed backward, her fingers sweaty and her arms aching. Despite the pain, she knew she'd made progress. The bottom hinge was loose now, meaning the whole door was weakened.

Carrie whistled a short, cheerful tune to herself as she surveyed her progress. A modern hinge, made in her own time and her own world, would have required special tools to take apart. Her gamble that this medieval-seeming world didn't have the same level of technology had paid off. Moreover, despite her non-magical nature, she had escaped by using a wand.

"I guess there's more than one way to be a sorceress," she chuckled.

After allowing herself the short celebration, she got back to work. She wanted very much to take a break, but she couldn't risk that Melania would come back and find her half-escaped. Then she really would be in distress.

Luckily, with one hinge loose, the rest of her job became easy. She put all her weight against the bottom half of the door and felt the entire thing shift slightly. Once again, the crack she'd been working on widening was large enough for her to slip her fingers into, but this time, the crack ran all the way up to the top hinge. Keeping her weight against the door, she started working this hinge in the same way she had the last. The metal pin that held it together dropped to the ground, turning the door into nothing more than a flat wooden hatch.

Unfortunately, the realization that the top hinge had come loose came while she was still leaning against the door with all her weight. Carrie tumbled forward with the door beneath her, landing hard in the hallway with an enormous bang that echoed throughout the castle. She got back on her feet again in seconds and let out a triumphant cheer despite herself, having tasted freedom for the first time in what seemed like ages.

The hallway she found herself in branched off in three different directions. Taking a quick look down each corridor, they too had multiple branches. She had escaped a cell only to find herself trapped in a maze.

"So you've escaped," Melania said, seeming to melt out of the shadows left by the flickering torches that lined the halls. "But you could have done it so much more easily if you were able to cast a simple spell."

Carrie's stomach twisted itself into knots. Had Melania been expecting her to do this? Could Carrie surprise somebody who controlled the shadows themselves?

"Yeah, well . . . bye!" Lacking any more lies, Carrie decided to go with her next plan: running as fast as she could.

"Do you really think you stand a chance?" Melania called. "If you had just been honest with me in the first place, you wouldn't be hunted right now!"

The enchantress closed her eyes and waved her hands. The hallway darkened, and the shadow-men who'd kidnapped her earlier appeared out of nowhere. At first, Carrie prepared to let her momentum carry her right into the creatures, hoping to plow right through them. But they raised their swords, and she stopped short, shaking as she realized that they might strike to kill this time.

"I can make an army to hunt you down," Melania said. "And if you do manage to find your way out of this castle, you'll find yourself lost in a city where every single person is completely loyal to me."

The shadow-men advanced upon Carrie, their swords raised.

"Or . . ." Melania said, and as she spoke, the attackers stopped mid-stride as though somebody had just hit the pause button on some sort of magical remote. "You can give up now. I won't make you return to your cell. I'll show you all the luxuries a queen possesses." She held out a slender hand. "I really do want a friend, Carrie."

Carrie looked at the shadow-men, standing stock still like they were frozen in time. If she refused Melania's offer and continued with her desperate escape attempt, those creatures would probably cut her to ribbons.

She sighed. The choice was obvious to her.

"Sorry," she said, "but you don't earn friends through threats."

Picking a corridor that she hoped would take her away from her pursuers, Carrie started running.

Thirteen

One of the problems with parents was they never appreciated it when you saved their lives. For nearly fifteen minutes straight, Sarah's mom had been lecturing her about the supposedly needless risks she had taken.

". . . a million different things you could have done, but you picked the one area where you're weakest." Sarah was only half-listening by now, paying more attention to the different kinds of fungus that grew underground than what her mom had to say. "You had no idea how to use a sword, and you won out of sheer luck. What if you had missed when you threw your blade? Then you would have been defenseless and skewered. How would that have helped anybody?"

"I dunno . . . I'm sure I would have thought of something else."

"Like what?"

"My plan worked, so it doesn't really matter now, does it?"

Her mom sighed in exasperation and stormed to the front of the group where Etten served as their guide.

Despite their apparent willingness to rob innocent travelers, work with crazy gremlins, and fight children, the two rogue dwarves did seem to have at least a little honor in them. Or, more accurately, they probably didn't see much benefit in breaking their word once Sarah had given Kytar bruises on his shins that would probably last for weeks. Regardless of their reasoning, the dwarves had given back the companions' weapons and spellbooks, provided enough food to get through a day of travel, and agreed that Etten would serve as their guide through the tunnels. And it was all thanks to Sarah, even though her mom seemed less than grateful.

With Sarah's mom picking up her pace, Dax staying within sword's reach of Etten in case he tried anything funny, and Keeley rushing ahead to explore every nook and cranny she could find, Sarah found herself bringing up the rear . . . almost. Kay had been trailing behind her but now sped up enough so he was walking by her side.

"I like your mom," he said cheerfully.

"Well, that makes one of us."

"Oh, come on. You don't mean that. How many other parents would let their daughter rush off on an adventure like this, whether she was an enchantress or not?"

"She didn't let me. If I hadn't run through your portal first, she probably would have made me stay in my room."

"You say that, but she didn't make me send you back once we got here. She may be worried about your safety, but she also seems to trust you."

"Then she should stop rubbing my nose in everything I do, especially since I just saved everybody."

"No offense, but I heard your conversation just now. I don't think she was trying to rub your nose in anything."

"Then what was she trying to do?"

Kay cast a glance up ahead and lowered his voice so Sarah's mom wouldn't be able to hear the conversation. "I think she's scared."

"Well, we did nearly get eaten by gremlins and all."

"No, that's not it. She's familiar with the valley—she knows the risks. But when she was here last, she was in your place. She was the plucky young lady out to save the valley from . . . oh boy, I don't remember my history very well. Boggarts, maybe?"

"What are boggarts?"

"Oh, they're nasty little spirits that live in swamps and kidnap people, and they worked for a witch some years back who . . . You know, I really need to read more often so I can get my facts straight." Kay shook his head, hopefully clearing some of the cobwebs out. "But that's not the important thing. What *is* important is your mom saved us from a *lot* of bad stuff. But that was all when she was a girl. She's a mom now. That means she has to be more responsible, right? So now, she's got to be thinking in the back of her head that she's being a terrible parent, letting you take these risks and all."

"But I'm not a kid. I'm practically an adult."

"Yeah, but it also wasn't that many years ago that you were in diapers. I mean, thirteen years seems like a long time to us—it's practically our whole lifetimes—but it's not that long ago for an adult. I mean, for your mom and Dax, it's . . . hm. How old do you think Dax is, anyway?"

"Eighteen," Sarah said. "The stress probably turned his hair gray and gave him all those wrinkles."

"Nah, he couldn't be that young, because he knew your mom, and she hasn't been in the valley since . . . Oh, I get it. A joke." Kay laughed much more loudly than Sarah thought her quip deserved. "I've missed you."

The cavern where the gremlins had captured them was only wide enough for two or three of them to walk abreast, and Sarah could have stood on her tiptoes and touched the ceiling. Deeper down where they were now, the tunnel seemed to be large enough to hold an entire village if enough people wanted to live there. Even with the light of Etten's torch, she could barely see the dark, gray stone of the ceiling up above. The immense tunnel seemed unusually round, with walls that were rather smooth, as though they were walking through a path made by some humongous earthworm. She shuddered and decided not to think too much about what kind of creature could actually have made something this big just by passing through.

The vast caverns gave off echoes that seemed to go for miles. A cough or shout got bounced back to them dozens of times, and their footsteps made their tiny band sound like an army. Above all else, though, Sarah heard the tapping of Kay's staff. The boy emphasized each footstep with a loud tap that, combined with the other echoes of the tunnel, started to grate on Sarah's nerves.

"Kay, would you cut that out?" she finally barked.

Kay blinked in confusion. Then, realizing what Sarah was talking about, he lifted the staff and slung it over his shoulder, ending the tapping.

Feeling a pang of guilt, Sarah asked, "Why do you do that?"

"I just like the feel of the staff in my hand, you know? It makes me feel more like a proper wizard."

"No, that's not what I meant. Why do you always go along with everything I say, even when I'm being mean or rude?"

"I know you don't mean it."

Sarah shook her head as though Kay's words were poison in her ears. "That's terrible logic. Since you found me in my world, I've punched you, yelled at you, and come very close to having a gremlin shoot you in the face! You should fight back more."

"First," Kay said, counting his reasons on his fingers, "you punched me because you didn't recognize me and thought I was being a creep. Second, the yelling . . . well, no offense, but you tend to be naturally crabby, especially after a battle. As to the gremlin . . . I knew you had a plan."

"You really trust me that much?"

"Of course I do. After all, it worked out, didn't it?"

Sarah had to nod in agreement with that, but her mom's scolding seemed to make more sense now. What if it hadn't worked out? Her fight with the beast-men had resulted in Dax getting hurt, all because of one stray arrow. Had anything gone wrong in the battle against Kytar, Kay probably wouldn't be here having this conversation with her.

Seeing the angst on her face, Kay put a friendly hand on Sarah's shoulder. "If it makes you feel so bad, I'll tell you what: next time you yell at me, I'll yell right back."

Sarah forced a crooked smile. "Look, it's just . . . memory problems or not, it seems like I haven't been fair to you. Why would you even tolerate somebody who treats her friends like that?"

Another thought occurred to her: How fair had she been lately to Carrie? How many times had she skipped watching her dance recital or made fun of her latest crush on a boy? She'd been blaming Melania and those shadow monsters for kidnapping Carrie, but what if Sarah hadn't tried hard enough to save somebody who once had been as close as a sister?

"Well," Kay said, "let's put it this way: I've been on my own for a long time, and I know what it feels like when other people don't give any thought at all to my feelings. Whatever you do, I know you'll think about how it makes me feel."

"Well, maybe I could start thinking about that a little bit earlier."

Kay grinned. "You won't hear me complaining if you do."

Sarah touched the hand on her shoulder and gave it a friendly squeeze. "Do you think my mom knows I don't mean it when I snap at her, either?"

"I don't know, but you could probably ask her."

Sarah glanced at her mom, who had slowed down a little bit and was closer to the two teenagers than they realized. She glanced back at Sarah, smiled, and nodded her head.

"If you don't mind, we're going to take a slight detour," Etten said when they reached a fork in the tunnel. The tunnel shifted in two directions—one was as huge and cavernous as the passageway in which they'd been traveling, while the other tapered off into a narrower corridor. The latter was still large enough to fit a horse through if they needed to, but not a parade of elephants like the area they'd traveled through for the last few hours.

Etten pointed down the larger tunnel. "That way leads to a dwarven city where, ah, let's say that a few of my more larcenous activities have led my kindred to take a dim personal view of my partner and I." He pointed down the narrower part of the fork. "This one has more twists and turns and such, but it will get us where we need to go almost as quickly and with fewer arrests."

"That sounds fine to Keeley!" the tiny dragon said as she zipped around the group. "The big tunnel has lots of interesting rocks and mushrooms, but the dwarves do not like even tiny, pretty dragons like Keeley! Although . . ." She hovered in front of Etten's face with a trail of smoke coming out of her nostrils. ". . . she isn't fond of smelly dwarves who think it might be fun to tie up Keeley and her friends either."

Etten sweated visibly under the dragon's harsh emerald stare. "I assure you, dear, ah . . . dragon . . . I feel nothing but the deepest regret for tying you up. And that feeling will only become more regretful if you do what I'm worried you're thinking of doing and set me on fire."

The smoke stopped trailing from Keeley's nostrils, and she gave a happy yip. "No, Keeley isn't going to set you on fire. She just wanted an apology!"

The dragon flew to the top of the dwarf's head and gave his ear a playful nip.

"Okay then," Etten said, wiping sweat from his brow. "Let's continue on our way."

Sarah and her companions quickly found that Etten was downplaying the number of twists and turns that the alternate route took. Every few feet, the passageway branched off in a different direction. The main route they followed had no rhyme or reason, sometimes shifting upward and sometimes sloping so sharply downward that it seemed like they were never going to find their way up to the surface. The sharp turns made Etten's torchlight almost ineffective. Even Keeley stayed closer to the group, unwilling to risk getting lost in the giant maze.

"Are you sure we're going in the right direction?" Sarah's mom asked after she noticed Etten slowing his pace and muttering to himself as they passed each new tunnel.

"Of course I do," Etten said, making sure to avoid eye contact as he spoke. "Remember, I live down here."

"Then you won't mind telling us how much farther we have to go?"

Etten stopped moving and swept his torch back and forth, taking a long look in every direction before answering. "We're almost there," he said. "The passage widens in a little bit. We'll reach a cave, and that cave will lead us right beneath the Great City. This area was dug out by rebels during the Dethroning War. This passageway fit their needs perfectly—it led them to the catacombs beneath the city, and all the confusing tunnels made it almost impossible for the king's soldiers to track them down."

"Then why are you shaking?"

"It's been a while since I've eaten. I get shaky when I'm hungry."

"Mm-hm." Sarah's mom nodded to Dax, who put a hand on the hilt of his sword. Sarah gripped her wand.

"Yes . . . well, let's continue," the dwarf said, trying his best to ignore the subtle threats.

True to Etten's prediction, the tunnel did expand again dramatically, leading to a large cavern that almost matched the size of the passageway they'd just come from. Two notable things made this cavern different from the others they'd seen. First was the smell of cooked meat, which made Sarah's stomach grumble. Second was a large pile of gold, silver, and gems that rose in a mound at the center of the cave.

"Oh, good," Etten said, relaxing a little as they entered the area. "He's not here."

"Who isn't here?" Sarah asked.

"Not important," the dwarf declared cheerily. "What is important is that we get out of here quickly." He pointed to an exit on the far side. "That passageway will lead us right to the Great City."

"Aren't you even the least bit interested in the mound of riches right there?" Sarah's mom asked. "I thought you cared more about money than anything else."

"No, madam. I care more about my life than anything else."

Keeley landed on Sarah's shoulder, her back arched like she was a cat getting ready for a fight. "Keeley knows what lives here," she said. "It's one of her bigger cousins."

"Precisely!" Etten cried. "And that's why we need to move right—"

A rumble stopped the dwarf short. Smoke curled out of one of the larger passageways and was followed by a long, green snout that looked like the mouth of a crocodile . . . but much bigger. Following the snout came the rest of the creature—a scaly green dragon that was almost the size of Sarah's house.

The dragon spotted them immediately. His mouth curled into a toothy grin.

"Why, thank you, Etten," it said. "It looks you've brought me some very interesting prey."

Fourteen

"**Y**ou're more afraid of a bunch of dwarves than a dragon?" Kay asked Etten angrily.

Etten looked helplessly between the companions and the green-scaled dragon. "This is . . . well, embarrassing isn't quite the word I would use," Etten said. "More . . . ashamed that I made a bad gamble."

"What gamble?" the dragon asked. "You and I had a deal, didn't we?"

"You planned this?" Sarah forgot about her spells for a moment and prepared to just punch Etten.

"The dragon is allied with Melania," the dwarf said. "The witch above knows about this passageway and found a guardian she thought nobody could get by. Of course, she didn't count on his appetite—he's usually out hunting for food. However, one time my partner and I happened across this cave at the wrong time . . ."

"You made me a deal," the dragon said. "I let you live, and you promised to bring others to me, so . . ." The dragon let his voice trail off and clacked his jaws. "Are you going to keep your word, little dwarf? Dragons always keep theirs, and we don't look kindly upon those who go back on their debts."

"Keeley knows you," the tiny dragon growled from atop her perch on Sarah's shoulder. "You're cousin Grimjaw. Adlin the dragon queen exiled you!"

Grimjaw squinted his eyes. "Well, well . . . little Keeley. And your friends. I remember the old man who looks too stringy and the boy in purple who needs to get fattened up before I fry him. And you have some new people too. A succulent-looking adult and . . ." The dragon's voice trailed off in confusion. His eyes widened, and his snout twitched as he sized Sarah up.

"Remember me?" Sarah grinned at the dragon's bewilderment.

"I . . . I . . ." Then, Grimjaw shook his head, apparently forgetting what he was trying to remember. "All food looks the same to me."

"Keeley's friends are not food." Sarah's tiny friend left her shoulder and landed on the ground a few feet from Grimjaw's front claws. It looked like a mouse trying to frighten a dinosaur. "These people are under Keeley's protection. That means you can't harm them, Grimjaw."

The larger dragon's lips curled cruelly. "Oh, can't I?"

"No! Dragons must honor the word of other dragons! It is ancient law!"

"Little Keeley, you weren't there when Adlin cast me out. She said I couldn't be trusted, that I had proven to be a threat to all other dragons. I would have shown her how much of a threat I really was if that big oaf Azal hadn't been right there to protect her. They sent me aboveground where the dragon hunters dwell. They took my treasures away and collapsed my lair." Grimjaw's voice raised to a roar that shook the caverns. "And the moment they did *that*, their words and their laws stopped meaning anything to me!"

The smaller dragon refused to back down. "Keeley doesn't care what they mean to you, Grimjaw. She still honors the pact, and she won't let you hurt her friends!"

"Little one, I have no wish to harm you. But you need to under-stand. I traveled the mountains for months, hunted by knights and centaurs who thought they could make a name for themselves by pierc-ing my hide. Then Melania found me. She gave me a new home, new treasures. In return, I promised to serve her. I care about that oath more than any pact formed by kin who turned their backs on me. Fly back through the tunnels you came through, Keeley. Take these humans if you must. But if any of you takes another step toward the Great City, I will gnaw on your cooked bones."

Keeley refused to budge. Grimjaw sighed.

"Do you really think you stand a chance against me, little Keeley?"

In answer, Keeley breathed in deeply. The column of flame she spat out covered Grimjaw's entire body, creating a wall of fire that lit the cavern up like daylight. The burst of brightness took almost every-thing the dragon had out of her, and she fell over onto her side. Sarah rushed forward and grabbed Keeley, sheltering her in the palms of her hands.

"Everyone!" her mom yelled. "Run for the exit!" She lifted her wand, preparing to cover their escape, pausing only to glare at Etten. "But you can roast for all I care."

Roaring in pain and anger, Grimjaw beat the leathery wings at his side until the flames that clung to his scales had been extinguished. His jaws snapped toward Dax, but he pulled back as a sharp blade came dangerously close to cutting off his tongue.

"I apologize, madam, I truly do." Etten stepped toward the angry Grimjaw, rummaging through his pockets as he did so. "Kytar would be ashamed of me. It was supposed to be a simple choice—bring you to the city if Grimjaw wasn't home, give you up if he was. But it never seems to be that easy, does it?"

Grimjaw dove toward the dwarf, ready to snap him up in his jaws. Etten produced a pair of the egg-like smoke bombs his gremlins had used. With a deep breath, he threw both of them right down the drag-on's throat.

The puff of yellow smoke engulfed Grimjaw's head and sent him into a fit of roars and coughs. Unfortunately, they didn't seem to be enough to fill the gigantic dragon's lungs the same way they had with Sarah and her companions. Grimjaw sent out a puff of fire, burning away the mist. He jumped into the air, shaking his head and hitting his skull against a stalactite.

With a wave of her wand, Sarah's mom filled the air around Grim-jaw with a thick, green cloud of smoke that clung around his face. She waved Sarah and Kay forward, then started following them in a frantic rush away from the dragon.

Sarah started pulling ahead but then stopped short as she found that Dax was lagging behind. He'd paused long enough to take a swipe at Grimjaw's leg with his sword. Closing his eyes tightly so he wouldn't see the spray of blood, the warrior nodded when he heard the dragon's roar of agony. Then he ran as well, but his wound still slowed him down.

After a few steps, he winced and stumbled. Sarah saw fresh blood soaking through his tunic and realized his bandages had come loose. She handed the wounded Keeley to Kay and reversed direction, run-ning for Dax. To her surprise, Etten also backtracked to the old warrior and got to him before she did. As Grimjaw spat out another burst of flame to burn away the fog, Sarah and the dwarf helped Dax back to his feet.

"This really is the stupidest thing I've ever done," Etten said.

"Don't worry," Dax said, moving as quickly as his wound would allow. "If you stick with us for a little while more, you'll see plenty of stupider things."

Sarah's mom stood firm until her daughter had passed her. Then she shouted more magic words and followed, defending the rear. Although Sarah didn't dare look behind her, she heard the spell's effect just fine—a mud-like squelching as the rocky ground the companions had just crossed turned into quicksand.

By the time Sarah, Dax, and Etten reached the others, Grimjaw had sunk all the way down past his front claws. His treasure had fallen into the sinking pit with him. The disappearance of his carefully collected gold made the dragon's snout tremble in rage.

"None of you are going to get out of these tunnels alive!" the dragon bellowed. "None of you!"

"We need to run faster," Dax said with a grunt. The warrior shifted his weight so neither Sarah nor Etten were supporting him anymore. He shoved both of them forward, urging them to follow the others. Then, gritting his teeth, he sped up, almost outdistancing both of them. Sarah quickened her pace, and her heart soared as she saw that they were heading toward a tunnel with a much lower ceiling—an area where Grimjaw's size wouldn't let him follow them.

Unfortunately for the companions, Grimjaw was more determined than ever to chase them down. Beating his wings frantically, he sprayed quicksand across the cavern, eventually taking flight and pulling himself out of the pit. He rushed the smaller cavern without slowing down and used his powerful front claws to break through rock, digging his way after the group.

"This way!" Kay shouted as he waved toward one of the branching tunnels.

Whether Kay was following some wizard's intuition or just guessing, Sarah never found out if his decision would have led them true. A tremor caused by Grimjaw's digging split the ceiling, causing the tunnel to collapse. Kay threw himself backward and shielded Keeley with his body, then disappeared in the cloud of dust caused by the falling debris.

"Follow me!" Etten said, pushing his way to the front of the group and running alongside Sarah before taking a sharp turn down a different tunnel.

"Shut up!" Sarah shouted. "We're never trusting anything you ever say again!" She rushed for Kay, reaching him as the dust settled.

"I'm okay, I think," Kay said as he got to his knees. He handed Keeley over to Sarah, picked up the hat that had fallen off his head, and tried to get going at a run again . . . only to pull up short and wince. "Except my ankle feels like it's on fire," he amended.

Sarah and her mom exchanged hopeless looks. Running through the tunnels with a wounded Dax was one thing. Trying to do so when Keeley was unconscious and Kay could barely move made their escape nearly impossible.

"There's no getting around it," her mom said. "We need to stand and fight."

"You fools!" Etten snapped. The dwarf glared at them sourly but didn't run away like Sarah thought he would. "You might as well serve yourselves up on a platter!"

A rush of air filled the tunnel as Grimjaw took in a deep breath. Holding Keeley with one hand, Sarah fumbled for her wand with her other, realizing that the companions were doomed if Grimjaw breathed fire in the tunnel. Unfortunately for everybody involved, Kay was the first person to utter the words to a spell.

"Don't worry!" the boy shouted. "A wall of stone should save the day . . . *Veda aquea trux*!"

Kay did summon up a wall . . . just not one made of stone. Instead of fire filling the cavern, the companions found themselves surrounded by steam. The water that Kay had created did manage to douse the dragon's flame, but it didn't stop there. It filled the entire passageway, creating a flash flood that rushed toward the group.

Sarah quickly found herself pulled underwater and carried along with a current like a stick in a stream. She banged her shoulder hard on a stalactite that sent her crashing against the rocky wall before the water carried her carelessly down its path at a dangerous speed. She kicked her legs, trying to get some sort of control even though both hands remained clutched tightly around Keeley's body. It did no good. Even though she was a very good swimmer, she couldn't control herself, given the speed of the current.

She didn't dare to look behind her for fear that one of her companions had already been swept down an unseen side tunnel and lost forever. Worse, she was running out of air. Her lungs burned, and her body ached from all the bangs and bruises she had taken along the way.

Then, just as everything was starting to fade to black, she felt arms pulling her to safety. The tunnel sloped upward, and the waters calmed. Her mom and Dax worked together to pull her onto dry land. As soon as she cleared the water, Keeley wriggled from her grasp, coughing and sputtering. The gags and sneezes might have resulting in bursts of flame had the dragon not been so waterlogged. Instead, tiny rings of steam rose from around her nose and mouth.

As her vision cleared, Sarah found herself in a cavern that was definitely manmade, with smooth walls and sculptures carved into stone arches that supported the roof. Without Etten's torch, the light filtered in through grates in the ceiling. That light was true, golden sunlight—something Sarah thought she might never see again.

"Is everyone here?" Kay asked from further up the tunnel. Sarah turned her head to see him limping slightly as he checked on each companion in turn. "Good," he said. "Looks like we're all okay . . . and so is Etten."

"Okay?" Sarah shouted. "We almost drowned back there. When will you learn to keep your spells under control?"

"Hey!" Kay replied in an equally angry tone. "They don't always work, but they do what needs to get done, and this time it worked out even better than I had planned! A stone wall would have taken Grimjaw all of a second to break through, but the water got us out of there faster than he could follow. So instead of yelling at me, why don't you thank me for a change?"

Sarah blinked, stunned at her friend's anger.

Kay stopped his tirade and broke into a smile. "See? I promised you I'd yell back at you the next time you snapped at me. How'd I do?"

Sarah couldn't help but laugh. "Marvelous. Simply marvelous."

Etten let out a shrill yell that reminded Sarah of his partner Kytar. A look at the dwarf told her the source of his problem: Keeley was perched on his bulbous nose, her teeth bared menacingly.

"Keeley definitely doesn't like nasty men who try to feed her friends to dragons," she hissed. "She should burn off your eyebrows."

"Don't, Keeley." It seemed like something her mom would say, but surprisingly, the voice belonged to Sarah.

"Why not?" the little dragon asked.

"Because we don't have time to waste on him right now. And he did help us against Grimjaw, even if he was the one who put us in danger in the first place." Sarah extended her hand to help the dwarf to his feet while Keeley flapped up to her shoulder. "Why did you do that, anyway?"

"I'm . . . not sure, really. I had this strange feeling when I thought about the fact that I had just lured you nice people into a dragon's lair. It was . . . hm, how do I explain it? It was like I regretted the decision I had made, but not because it lost me money."

"Do you mean you felt guilty?"

"Guilt-ee?" The dwarf rolled the word around his tongue as though it were a completely foreign notion to him. "I guess that would be it. Whatever it was, it certainly wasn't an enjoyable feeling."

"Do you know where we are now?" Sarah's mom asked, wringing the water out of her long brown hair.

"This? These are the catacombs beneath the Great City. Hundreds of dead soldiers and nobles lie entombed deeper down these tunnels. They were supposedly placed here to help defend against the great demon Choronzon. In fact, some people say the dead still walk . . ."

"They may walk," Dax said, "but we won't. Not very far anyway, given our wounds."

Etten frowned and reached into his satchel, which had somehow remained at his side. He silently took stock of his supplies, frowning in dismay as he found out how extensively waterlogged his gear was.

"Maybe we won't have to go far," Sarah's mom said. "Everybody stay here for a moment. I'll see if I can find a place for us to rest safely."

Too tired even to argue with her mother, Sarah flopped to the ground and took long, deep breaths. Her chest hurt with every inhale, but it was a good kind of pain—the kind that told her she wasn't drowning.

She heard the clink of glass coming from Etten's pouch, followed by the dwarf quietly mumbling to himself.

"What are you looking for, anyway?" she asked.

"Well," Etten said, "I may happen to have something that can help—"

A shout from Sarah's mom interrupted the dwarf. "Sarah! Come here quickly!"

Her mom didn't sound frightened, but her tone was close enough to get Sarah on her feet and running. The rest of the companions rushed after her as quickly as their battered bodies could bring them.

Fifteen

It didn't take Carrie long to figure out that the shadow creatures were herding her away from any exits. They were content to let her try any door she came across as long as it didn't lead to the way out. When she got close to an area that looked like an exit route, they rose out of darkness and drew their swords, forcing her to stop on a dime and dash in the opposite direction. Pretty soon, the walls and paintings within the massive castle all ran together, leaving her well and truly lost.

All the while, Melania's voice stayed in her ear. "It's pointless to run, Carrie. You don't have to go back to your cell. Just give up, stay with me, and I'll make sure you're comfortable and happy. You won't even remember the concept of pain."

Sometimes, she saw her captor following her. Other times, the voice seemed to come from nowhere at all. Regardless of where it was coming from, it kept repeating itself—especially the last part. Carrie shuddered at the thought of not remembering pain. Melania seemed to think she was making a good offer, but the idea of taking the bad parts of her life away still seemed . . . Invasive was the only word she could think of to describe the feeling.

She noticed something else as she ran through the castle: it was huge, easily bigger than any house Carrie had ever been in before. Despite that, it was empty except for Melania and the people she conjured up.

Carrie reached a great central staircase and dashed down the steps two at a time, nearly tripping over the red carpet at one point. She caught herself on the polished oak railing and made it down to the lower landing. The large balcony had more stairs leading down to a ground floor, two doors leading to other chambers, and a large stained-glass window that displayed a woman in green robes fighting a dragon. Somebody had gone through a lot of effort to scratch up the glass, leaving the woman's face unrecognizable.

She heard footsteps coming up the stairs and saw a pair of shadow creatures. She started to dash to the left, only to find more of Melania's minions blocking the doorway. She turned to the right and saw the same obstacle. Looking up, she saw Melania standing at the top of the staircase. The conqueror of Greystone Valley beckoned with one hand, crooking a finger and calling to her quarry.

"There's nowhere left to go," her captor said. "I admire your fire, but warriors and wizards have fought against me to no avail. In the end, they all learned how foolish they were."

Carrie shuddered. Melania's words made it seem like she was going to reach into Carrie's mind and change her thoughts. Could she do that? If she could, how long would it take? Sarah's spells always seemed to happen instantly. Then again, Sarah had never summoned up shadow people before.

Whether Melania could control minds or not, Carrie decided she couldn't risk finding out. She saw only one way out, so she took it.

She dashed toward the stained glass window. Only at the very last moment did she realize that maybe windows didn't break as easily as they did in the movies she'd seen, but by then, she didn't have time to stop herself. She put her arms in front of her to protect her head and leapt toward the damaged part of the glass, plunging straight into the green enchantress's scratched-out face.

True to her suspicions, the window didn't shatter easily. In fact, had she not leapt for the damaged part, she might have just bounced off and looked foolish. Instead, the glass split open in three large shards. Carrie's momentum carried her through the window, but the broken shards tore at her clothes and cut into her sides like long knives. She cried out with a gasping, sobbing sound she knew didn't sound very heroic. However, how she sounded was the least of her worries. Even the fact that she was now bleeding wasn't her biggest concern. Right now, she had to worry about the fact that she was plummeting to her doom.

The world spun as she dropped rapidly toward the cobbled stone road below. Fortunately, luck was on her side for a change. Rather than hitting the ground, she landed in the back of a horse-drawn carriage carrying loosely tied bales of hay that had been moving through the street. This gave her something of a cushion for her fall, but she still landed hard enough to sink deep into the hay and crack the wood at the bottom of the wagon. The breath left her lungs, and everything went black for a split second.

Stars floated in front of her eyes, but then her vision cleared. The wagon had stopped at the sudden impact of her body landing in the back. The driver stared at her as she pulled herself free of the hay and tumbled out of the cart.

Up above, Melania looked through the broken window, staring angrily at the bleeding girl in the streets below.

"You have to help me!" Carrie shouted to the driver. "I've been held prisoner!"

At first, she was sure the driver would help her. After all, who wouldn't come to the rescue of a young girl who was obviously hurt, scared, and in need of a hero? But then she looked into the man's face, and hope evaporated from her heart like water in a desert.

The bearded man wore a simple brown tunic and had a wide-brimmed hat that kept the sun out of his eyes. Those eyes, Carrie saw, were vacant. His face was blank and almost emotionless. Almost, but not quite. A slight smile showed on his lips— a stupid, vacant smile that told Carrie that there were no real thoughts behind it.

The Great City had streets full of bustling people, ranging from merchants in small outdoor shops to tourists who couldn't stop looking up at the tall buildings that apparently didn't exist in their homeland. Carrie turned in a circle and shouted for help, hoping that somebody would come to her rescue. But they all had the same smile on their faces.

"There is an escaped prisoner in your midst!" Melania shouted from her broken tower window. "Bring her to me!"

All at once, the people of the Great City turned toward Carrie and reached out to grab her. They acted almost like zombies but moved just as quickly as normal people. Soon, she was running again, but not from a witch and her shadow puppets. Now an entire city wanted to bring her back to her prison.

She did her best to ignore the pain that lingered after her fall, but it still slowed her down. One hand managed to get hold of her hair. She forced herself blindly forward, ignoring the pain as a handful of her blonde hair ripped right out of her head. She got to the end of the street and stumbled. She'd run less than a hundred feet, and her body already wanted to give up.

"You've got to do this," she whispered to herself. "Nobody's going to save you unless you save yourself." Then she ran faster than before, twisting and dodging as people came inches away from grabbing her.

The city had seemed small and idyllic from her window high up in the tower, but now she saw that it was bustling with people. The streets were full of crowds and wagons, carts, and shops, with no apparent way out.

She needed to get out of the streets somehow. Her mind ran on autopilot, scanning each building and alleyway for a possible exit. Finally, her frantic dash led her down a twisted alleyway that allowed her to slip out of sight from her pursuers. She heard a crowd of people not far behind her and looked about desperately for a place where she could hide.

A few yards away, she saw an old, run-down wooden house. The door was unlocked and partially ajar. Carrie hesitated at first, worried that it might be a trap. But she didn't have any other clear escape route, so she rushed inside and hoped for the best.

The house was a simple, small building with no glass in the windows and furniture that looked to have been abandoned long ago. If anybody lived here, they hadn't been around for a few years at least.

She slammed the door behind her but knew it wouldn't hold. In fact, it looked like the lock had broken long ago. A ladder led upstairs to an attic, and a door led downstairs to a cellar. She chose to go down. That way, at least she wouldn't have to jump out a window again.

The cellar floor was made of wood, but given how far the planks had rotted, dirt would have worked just as well. She listened carefully for a very long moment, hoping that her pursuers had run past the house. For a long moment, it seemed like they had. But then she heard footsteps—just a few people, but enough to indicate that her hiding place wouldn't remain safe for very long.

Despair gave way to frustration, and Carrie stamped her feet angrily, furious at the knowledge that she'd gone through all that trouble only to wind up trapped like a rat in a cage. Then she got lucky for the second time that day. Unfortunately, her luck always seemed to come with painful falls.

As she stomped her foot on the brittle wood with a sob of aggravation, the floor gave way. Suddenly, she found herself tumbling down a deep hole. The rush through blackness only took a second, but it felt like she fell a hundred feet or more. She hit the ground hard and blacked out.

She was glad when she woke up in a dreary, dimly lit cavern rather than a comfortable room with fruit on the table and bars on the windows. She felt woozy as she stood up. Her arms shook, her vision was blurry, and she felt like everything around her was spinning out of control.

Through the haze and confusion of her agony, she heard footsteps above her. She must have been out only briefly—the people who'd entered the abandoned house were only just now getting to the basement. Hopefully, nobody who saw the hole would be foolish enough to jump blindly down it in pursuit of her. Carrie didn't want to stick around and find out, though. She got up and kept running, even though it was quite hard to do so without any light or a real sense of direction. She felt along rough stone walls, stepping as quickly as possible and hoping she would find a place with some light soon.

She fled down the tunnel until her body couldn't take it anymore. Finally, her knees buckled and she hit the ground. She tried pushing herself up onto her feet again but only had the strength to roll onto her back. Even when she heard footsteps approaching, she couldn't bring herself to move. If she didn't die from her wounds, she'd be Melania's prisoner again soon—a mindless slave masquerading as a friend to the enchantress. As she gave up hope completely, the only thing she could think of was that she missed having a real friend.

"Sarah! Come here quickly!"

That name . . . could it be? Part of her feared that this was another trick from Melania. After all, even with all of her magic, Sarah couldn't make it into another world . . . could she?

Suddenly, a green-clad enchantress entered her view, dispelling any doubts Carrie had.

"Carrie?" Sarah had a smile on her face—a real smile, brought from a hope realized, and not one of those fake things the people in the city wore.

At first, Carrie didn't know how to respond. In her cell, she'd decided their friendship couldn't keep going even if they did see each other again. Now, though . . . had Sarah really traveled to another world to save her?

"Sarah?" she asked weakly.

In response, Sarah threw her arms around Carrie, giving her a long, heartfelt hug. Carrie let the questions swirling in her mind disappear for a moment. Despite her wounds, the pain and fear of the past two days vanished, if only for a moment.

Sixteen

udging from Carrie's appearance, Sarah guessed that her imprisonment had been worse than fighting beast-men, getting captured by gremlins, and nearly drowning while fleeing an angry dragon. In fact, nobody dared move her for fear of making things worse.

Her heart hammering harder with every second, Sarah finally broke the silence. "We've got a dragon behind us, who knows what in front of us, we're soaked to the skin, and half of us can barely move. I don't want to step on Dax's toes here, but I'd say we're doomed."

Dax opened his mouth to interject but then simply nodded in agreement.

Etten cleared his throat. "Why not just use a potion?"

Blood rushed into Sarah's ears, and for a moment she thought she might literally explode in frustration. "What do you mean use a potion?"

"Before our new guest arrived, I was about to say that I might have something useful here in my haversack."

"How useful?"

The dwarf unslung the sack around his shoulders and removed three rolled leather strips. Unwrapping each of them, he revealed a trio of small crystal vials filled with what looked like black ink.

"I was saving these in case things went badly for me against the dragon. They're fairly rare, so I hope you all appreciate the sacrifice I'm making for all of you."

"A sacrifice for us?" Sarah said. "Are you sure you're not just trying to hustle us out of here before Grimjaw finds out where the river took us?"

"I admit, that is also a consideration that is weighing heavily on my mind." Kytar handed one of the vials to Dax and pointed at Carrie. "Here . . . pour this potion onto the girl's wounds, and they should close. Make sure you clean them and remove the broken glass first."

Dax took one look at Carrie and immediately handed the vial over to Sarah. He bent over and put his head between his knees, unnerved by the sight of so much blood.

"You know, you're bleeding too," Sarah told Dax.

"Please," he whispered, "don't remind me."

Etten, for once, was as good as his word. The potions stopped Carrie's bleeding and helped close Dax's wound again. Etten used the third one to soak a wet strip of cloth and apply it to Kay's ankle. The swelling went down, and in a few moments, the boy was able to walk normally again.

"There," the dwarf said sourly. "That's the last of my potential life-saving elixirs. Now, since we're defenseless, low on supplies, and still in need of getting to safety, I suggest we—"

Carrie interrupted, grabbing Sarah and squeezing so hard that the youngest Emerald Enchantress thought she heard her bones groan.

"You came all the way into another world to find me! I didn't know your magic could do that. And your mom's here!" Her voice became more high-pitched from there. "And Mr. Daxon! You do have swords! And some sort of weird tiny man . . ."

"You could just call me Etten," the dwarf said grumpily.

"And . . ." Carrie looked at Kay. "You looked a lot more muscular in my . . ." She blushed. "Never mind."

"And Keeley!" said a tiny voice near her ear. Carrie jumped.

"Oh my!" Her voice was startled at first. Then she let out a high-pitched squeal. "You are literally the cutest thing I have ever seen!"

"I hate to interrupt this happy reunion with my usual gloomy news," Dax said, "but we desperately need to get some rest and take stock of our situation . . . preferably in a place that lies somewhere aboveground."

"If only we had a place where we could rest up," Sarah groaned in frustration.

Then she noticed that Etten was staring intently at his feet, hoping nobody would look in his direction.

"Oh my gosh!" Sarah exclaimed. "How much are you hiding from us?"

"It's not really hiding," the dwarf said. "It's just failing to mention certain things. Kytar and I have some hidden safe houses around here. We used them when we sold smuggled goods and needed a hiding place from the authorities. They haven't been as necessary lately, since Melania is much more lax on crime . . ."

"Because everybody up there is a brainwashed zombie!" Carrie shouted.

"Zombies or not, they pay money just like everybody else," Etten retorted. "And, as a sign of goodwill, I would be happy to take you to one of the houses . . . especially if you all stop looking like you're getting ready to break my arms."

Etten led the way, followed closely by Sarah's mom, who lit her wand to provide some extra light in addition to what filtered down through the grates above them. Etten directed her to shine the light down certain passageways as he navigated the branching tunnels ahead.

"You have to understand, my partner and I had a very lucrative business until rather recently," he said. "The easiest way from the northern mountains to the Great City is through our pass. We've done our best to make sure people have safe trips through in order to encourage that route. Then, when the gremlins get a bit too restless for us to control, we let them rob a few travelers. Coins and weapons we could keep or give to the gremlins, and the rest we would bring to one of our safe houses in the Great City. Once we got to the streets, we could sell the merchandise for a tidy profit as though we were the original owners. A few times, we even sold the same goods back to the people we stole it from."

"That has got to be one of the sleaziest things I've ever heard," Sarah said.

"You, my dear, must live a very sheltered life. Trust me, there's much worse out there. Anyway, this was all well and good for a while, but then Melania struck a bargain with Grimjaw and gave him the cave that we used to use as our way into the city." The dwarf sighed heavily. "Now I'm afraid my life of luxury may be over."

"You could always try working for a living," Sarah's mom said.

"Madam, you remind me very much of my own mother. A pity I didn't listen to her a little better."

The tunnel seemed to reach a dead end. Etten walked to the damp wall and rubbed the stone. Disguised almost perfectly under a thin layer of clay were ladder rungs that led about fifteen feet up. Etten was about to start climbing when he looked up and saw a hole in the ceiling of the cave.

"Hm," he said. "Looks like somebody else has been here. This place might be compromised. We'd better move on."

Carrie craned her neck and gasped. "Compromised? This is the place where I fell through the floor. You're telling me I could have used a ladder?"

"My dear, we use the clay to disguise the ladder specifically so people won't follow us if they find the secret passage. Had you uncovered that ladder, your pursuers probably would have caught up to you and prevented your rather touching reunion with young Sarah here." Etten took one more look upward before moving toward another tunnel branch. "Although I wish you had discovered the secret trap door. There was no reason to break through the floor like that."

Sarah and Carrie looked at each other. Then they both scowled at the dwarf.

Even though their wounds had been treated, the day's adventures left all of the companions more exhausted than usual. This meant more frequent breaks. On one of those breaks, Carrie pulled Sarah into a side passage where they could talk.

"What's wrong?" Sarah asked, bewildered by the nervous, almost sad expression on her friend's face.

Carrie nibbled at her lower lip for a moment, then threw her arms around Sarah. "I'm sorry."

"Sorry? For what?"

"Our last conversation . . . and the things I thought after that."

"You're sorry for your thoughts?"

"No. I'm sorry because I didn't think we were friends anymore. And when I was stuck in Melania's cell . . . well, I didn't want to be friends anymore."

Despite her confusion, Sarah felt a slight sting of hurt in her heart. "Why not?"

"I'm not like you. I'm not a sorceress, and I'm not comfortable running around and having these crazy near-death experiences you call adventures. I don't like the idea of running around chasing storms. I'd rather just listen to some music and sit in a bubble bath."

"Well, it's not like I enjoy getting attacked by monsters myself, but . . ."

"But what?"

Up until just then, Sarah had all but forgotten about the conversation they'd had just before Melania's minions attacked. Something had been bothering Carrie, and Sarah had let the matter drop. She saw now that Carrie's worries about their friendship weren't something that had been caused by the stress of her imprisonment—they were something they should have talked about long ago.

"But . . ." Sarah continued, pausing just a second to gather her thoughts. "But I don't like a lot of the things you're interested in either. I couldn't care less about dance recitals, and I wouldn't be caught dead wearing the frilly little skirts you wear to school sometimes. We've got a lot of differences between us, but there's only one real reason I came back to Greystone Valley, and it's not because of Melania. I mean, I'm sure I would have come back to help if Dax and Kay had asked me without you getting kidnapped first, but there was only one reason I literally ran through the portal into this world. I wanted to make sure you were okay."

"Really?" Carrie got that same misty-eyed look she got whenever she watched a sad movie, another habit of hers that often made Sarah roll her eyes, but one she suddenly found she didn't want to be without.

"I'd rather talk every day about how different we are than not talk at all," Sarah said. "I mean, we don't have to be clones of each other to still be friends, right? Friendship can just happen."

"I . . . yeah, I guess it can."

"Oh, and one more thing."

"What?"

"I'm sorry I got you dragged into the principal's office with me the other day at school."

Carrie hugged Sarah again. "Apology accepted."

Several hours later, the companions finally found themselves at another ladder leading up into the city. This time, the floor of the safe house didn't have a Carrie-sized hole in it.

"I'm sure none of you will mind, but this is where I say farewell," the dwarf said. "Going above the ground means stepping into the sunlight, and for a dwarf, that means a terrible sunburn and a beard that grows horrifically fast. I don't fancy the days it would take for me to shave my face, and I don't expect that any of you will mind that I'm not around to lead you into any more dragon lairs."

The faces of the companions softened as the larcenous dwarf seemed almost heartbroken to leave the group behind—or, more likely, he was realizing that this trip to the Great City hadn't netted him any sort of profit.

"I don't often make promises," Etten continued, "but I do keep them when they get made. I can personally guarantee you that our gremlins will make sure you pass through our tunnels unharmed from here on out. I know for a fact that Kytar probably doesn't want to deal with Sarah's wrath again. And as for the rest," he gave a low bow, "feel free to use the safe house for as long as you need. I can't say I wish you all that much luck against Melania, because her presence makes life easier for thieves like me. But . . . well, I won't feel terrible if you manage to overthrow her and force Grimjaw to leave my tunnels either."

Etten bowed once more, then shuffled off into the darkness.

Sarah almost asked out loud if the dwarf had really been all that bad. Then she remembered that he'd nearly gotten them killed by both gremlins and a dragon. Maybe it was best not to think of him too much, lest she decide to chase after him and give him a swift kick in the rear.

The safe house offered little in the way of luxury, but the companions were just happy to spend a few hours without something trying to capture them or eat them for a change. They emerged from their long excursion underground to find twilight setting in across the Great City. Through small shuttered windows, Sarah and Carrie watched as streetlamps ignited by themselves. They glowed blue-green and made the entire community look as though it were being bathed in the light of millions of fireflies.

"Nobody outside is even looking up when the lights come on," Sarah observed. "I guess they're all used to magic around here."

"I don't think it's that," Carrie replied. "There's something strange about this whole place. Everybody seems . . . well, happy, but it's like that's the only thought that ever comes into their heads."

Sarah looked out the window again and saw that her friend was right. The people outside seemed to be acting normally enough—merchants sold their wares, cleaners swept the gutters, and travelers strolled through the streets talking busily amongst themselves. But they all had a strange stupid grin on their faces, like everything they were doing was just part of a dream. None of them put any passion into their tasks. They were like puppets, moving along gracefully and without hesitation but still only going where the person pulling their strings told them to go.

"We need to figure out a way to take Melania down," Carrie said. "I think we should attack at dawn."

"No," Sarah said. "We need to get you home first. Keeley, do you think you would be able to get Carrie back to Castle Greystone?"

"Of course Keeley can do that! But remember, Keeley is a dragon, and dragons are forbidden to enter the castle. We would need somebody else to guide Carrie to the right door, yes we would!"

"Hm. Right. I hadn't thought of that."

"It doesn't matter anyway," Carrie objected. "I'm not going anywhere!"

"I thought you hated the idea of an adventure!"

"I do! Who wants to fight a stupid witch-queen when there's apparently a whole valley full of faeries and pretty things? But I'm also not about to let those people out there stay like that. If we're going to take down Melania, I'm going to help."

"Um, no offense Carrie, but I can cast spells to defend myself. So can my mom and Kay . . . sort of. Dax is an expert swordsman, and Keeley can breathe fire. I don't mean to sound harsh, but your only accomplishment in this world is getting captured."

"I got caught by surprise!" Carrie yelled. "That could happen to anybody! What, you've never been captured before, Miss Emerald Enchantress?"

Sarah opened her mouth to give a retort, then looked at the floor sheepishly. "Okay . . . you have a point."

Seventeen

After a restful night of sleep, Sarah woke up to the sound of steel ringing against steel.

The safe house was a simple one-story cottage with no real beds to speak of, just some dirty straw that none of the companions had wanted to sleep on. A single iron stove served as their fire for the night, and its heat drifted into the cramped attic that served as a bedroom. Waking up with a start, Sarah almost bumped her head against the wooden rafters before she remembered where she was and who she was with. She rushed down the ladder to find the companions already downstairs. Thankfully, the swordfight didn't involve any new attackers. Instead, it was between Dax and Carrie.

"Keep your back foot perpendicular to your front," the old warrior said as he took a dueling stance.

Carrie responded by pointing her front foot toward Dax and placing her back foot so it made a "T" shape against her heel. She then raised the smaller blade Dax had taken from one of Carrie's kidnappers.

"Oh . . . so that's what 'perpendicular' means," Sarah muttered as she reached the bottom of the ladder.

"Is this good?" Carrie asked.

"Not really. You're liable to get skewered that way. But it's not your fault. I always was a dreadful teacher." Dax moved to Carrie's side and repositioned her feet so they were about a shoulder's length apart. "There," he said, returning to his original spot. "Keep your stance wide, and you have a better chance of keeping your balance. Then your enemies won't be able to trip you—unless you're like me and constantly fall over your own feet."

Carrie beamed, shifting her weight experimentally. "It's like dancing," she said.

"Indeed," Dax said. "The skill set is the same." He looked at Sarah's mom, who was smiling in the corner with her arms crossed. "Although," he said ruefully, "I never was a very good dancer despite that fact."

"What's going on here?" Sarah asked.

"Dax is giving me sword fighting lessons!" Carrie twirled like a ballerina with a blade and gave an experimental thrust toward her mentor. With a sigh and a shake of his head, the old warrior flicked his wrist, sending Carrie's blade flying from her grasp.

"*Trying* to give sword-fighting lessons," Dax corrected her. "Although I must say that anybody who relies on me as a teacher is likely to wind up cut to ribbons by the time she enters her first battle."

Sarah went quiet and let her friend continue practicing. She'd never thought of Carrie as much of a fighter. She seemed more like the type of person who practiced painting, singing, or dancing, although seeing how quickly Carrie took to Dax's instructions, it now seemed obvious that sword fighting was just another kind of dancing to her. A part of Sarah hurt as she realized that Carrie had known more violence in the last couple of days than she had ever experienced in her entire life.

Dax started slowly, moving at about a quarter of his normal speed so Carrie could see the blows coming in time and block them. Carrie's first defensive moves looked like something from an action movie, where she used the blade like a shield and let Dax's sword ring against hers.

"You can't block like that very often," Dax said. He pointed to the edge of his own sword, which had a few nicks and scratches in it from frequent use. "Steel is strong, but a sword isn't invulnerable. If you block with the blade too much, you'll just wind up with a broken weapon."

"Then how am I supposed to do it?" Carrie asked.

"You don't block," Dax said. "You parry. Try to cut me."

"Are you sure about that, Dax?" Sarah interjected. "If Carrie does get lucky, the arrow wound you took will look like a scratch."

"I've had worse," he said. "And I'm certain I'll have worse again soon. Trust me, when you get old and broken down like I am, you get very used to pain."

Carrie lunged at Dax, moving with grace and speed that Sarah didn't expect. The old warrior barely exerted any energy in his defense—a flick of his wrist was all it took. Keeping his blade pointed at Carrie, he caught the inside of her sword and pushed it to the side. Carrie's lunge wound up coasting past Dax's body without so much as scratching him.

"See?" Dax asked. "Parrying requires less energy, so it keeps you fresher during the fight. It doesn't risk as much damage to your sword, and it means that you have a clear shot at your opponent." Dax tapped Carrie in the ribs with the side of his blade.

Carrie picked up these lessons quickly, and Dax soon went from quarter-speed to half-speed. Even moving slower than normal, however, the old warrior was hard to keep up with in combat. It took Carrie several tries before she finally managed to deflect one of Dax's sword strokes instead of getting tapped in the ribs with the flat part of his blade.

"Well done, Carrie," Kay said when that moment finally came.

Carrie fluttered her eyes at Kay and blushed. Then Dax took the distraction to knock the sword out of her hand.

"Oh well," she muttered. "Back to the drawing board, I guess."

Fencing practice was all well and good, but the companions had to worry about much more than getting Carrie up to speed. They took turns peering out of the small wooden shutters that looked into the streets, watching a city that didn't even know it needed to be liberated.

"This is stupid," Sarah muttered between small bites of sweetened porridge. "We've practically fought whole armies on our own before."

"Yeah," Kay said, "and if we were going out there just to pick a fight, we'd probably stand a good chance. It's mostly peasants out there, not soldiers. But I don't really feel comfortable tossing fireballs around a city full of people who sell bread and fish for a living."

"When you guys told us about Melania, I imagined she'd have an army waiting for us."

"She does," Kay responded. "It's just that her army is full of people whose thoughts she's manipulated and who's memories she's taken away. Do you want to go punch people in the face who don't really deserve it?"

"Why not?" Sarah joked. "I've done it before, haven't I?"

"Okay, good point. But remember that you still felt bad about that one after the fact."

Melania's castle stood several blocks away. Its single spire was smoother than the aged, craggy side of Castle Greystone and not nearly as tall, but it still towered above all the buildings of the Great City save for the clock tower in the distance. For some reason, Sarah got the uncomfortable feeling that both buildings had creatures inside that were ready for anything the companions had to challenge them with.

"Are we sure we really need to do something about Melania?" she asked. "If everybody's happy under her rule, should we be the ones to break them out of it?"

"Yes!" Carrie cried. "Happiness is a good goal, but it can't be everything in life. The things that make me mad or sad are also the things that make me want to do stuff. Those things are what add choices to our lives. Melania doesn't have any right to steal that from anyone."

"She took our memories of Greystone Valley away from us, sweetie," Sarah's mom said. "That's a lot of hiding underground, sleeping on rocks, and fighting monsters, but given the choice, would you have let her do that?"

"No, you're right," Sarah responded. "We obviously need to stop her, but I guess the problem is I have no idea how to do it. It would be a lot easier if we could just challenge her to a duel instead of letting her hide behind all those innocent people out there."

"What we need to do is find out what she really wants," Sarah's mom said. "Everybody we've run into has a motive: the beast-men wanted to be left alone, the gremlins wanted entertainment, Grimjaw wanted gold. Right now, Melania has an advantage over everyone. If we could figure out what makes her tick, we'd know how we can make her vulnerable."

"Keeley could find out!" The tiny dragon must have been getting restless, as she alternated between walking around the room on all fours and taking to the air to get some exercise. "She would sneak and peek and find everything Melania is hiding. Keeley's so small that nobody would find her while she was looking, oh no no no!"

"Actually," Sarah's mom said, "that might be our best bet . . ."

"She wants Sarah."

The rest of the companions looked at Carrie, who had spoken so quietly that her words almost didn't come out clearly. She was holding the sword Dax had given her, looking at her reflection in the polished blade.

"What do you mean?" Sarah asked.

Carrie jumped, as though she hadn't expected anybody to hear her. "Everything she's done so far is an attempt to capture Sarah for some reason. The shadow people took me by mistake—they thought they were kidnapping a sorceress. While I was imprisoned, I lied and said I could cast spells. She didn't believe me, but she seemed willing to let my lie play out for some reason. It was only when I escaped without using magic that she sprang her minions on me again. As long there was a chance that I might have been the sorceress, she didn't really treat me like an enemy. I don't know why, though."

Sarah's mom tapped her forehead. "That's what we need to figure out."

"We can figure it out when she's on fire," Sarah said. "This woman kidnapped my friend and brainwashed an entire city. She's got some payback coming."

"Sarah, be quiet."

"Come on, Mom!"

"Sarah, really—*be quiet!*"

Sarah got ready to snap, but then she realized what her mom was trying to say. When everybody in the safe house had stopped talking, the companions heard footsteps all around the building. The streets weren't the only source of the sound, though. People were on the roof—a lot of them. Down below in the basement, they heard creaking as well. The entire building was surrounded—around, above, and below.

"So, now we find the true sorceress," a young woman's voice said. From out of nowhere, a newcomer appeared in the room with them.

"Anya," Carrie said.

"It didn't have to be this way," Anya said sadly. "But I can't help you now."

Like a ghost, the girl disappeared. Then Melania's shadowy minions rushed into the building, leaving the companions trapped with nowhere to go.

Eighteen

In the blink of an eye, the companions found themselves fighting smoke. The creatures that swarmed loose into the building seemed to ignore walls, ceilings, and floors. The only difference between these monsters and actual smoke was the presence of claws and swords.

"We need to get outside, now!" Sarah's mom called.

Sarah knew her mom had the right idea, but she had other priorities first. She grabbed Kay by the hand and pulled him close to her. Then she grabbed Carrie and did the same.

"Kay, take care of her!"

"What?" Carrie yelled, raising the sword Dax had given her. "I can take of myself!"

"Fine, then watch our backs. But we're not going to let you get taken again!"

Carrie lunged forward with her sword, striking at one of the shadow creatures. The sword stroke missed wildly, but it forced the creature to take a step back and away from the companions. "Didn't you listen to anything I said? They're not after me—they're after you!"

Sarah's mom shouted the words to a defensive spell, creating a shining shield in midair that blocked her back as the shadow-creatures stabbed at her. Dax swung wildly with his sword. He struck with the flat of the blade right now, stunning his attackers and tripping them when he could. One such sword stroke didn't connect with anything solid—it just went right through the creature, causing it to burst into a puff of black smoke and disappear. Dax looked as shocked as everybody else.

"There's so many of them," Sarah said in realization. "She can't make them all real. The more there are, the less lifelike they become."

With this realization, Sarah tried to blind the attackers. If Melania made them from shadows, surely light would be their enemy. A bright flare filled the room, sending spots into her eyes and causing the shadow-creatures to reel in surprise. Unfortunately, Kay had the same idea, and that's when Sarah heard an all-too-familiar word from her friend . . .

"Oops."

The burst of light that came from Kay's staff burned brighter and hotter than Sarah's. It also came out with enough force to physically throw him out of the building. Since he was bunched up with Sarah and Carrie, he took them with him. The three friends shot toward one of the safe house's walls, and only some quick thinking and a rapid spell from Sarah blasted a hole large enough for all of them to pass through without getting crushed against the wood. That didn't slow down their eventual landing, though. They hit the cobbled streets and rolled, skinning their elbows and knees. But they had accomplished one important thing: they were outside now with more room to move.

It took Sarah two tries to get to her feet. Her eyes watered, and she could taste a mix of blood and gravel in her mouth. Despite that, her throat went dry when she looked back at the house. It was on fire, and her mom was still inside.

"Mom!"

She needn't have worried. It seemed that the original Emerald Enchantress was more than capable of taking care of herself, especially with her daughter free of the battle.

The fire froze. It didn't just stop—it literally *froze*, the tongues of flame instantly transforming into jagged blue ice. Then, with a crack, that ice broke. Dozens of the shadow creatures fell to the ground, their bodies covered in snow. The ice immediately took a new form, transforming into a wreath of green fire that formed an aura around her mom as she stepped free of the ruined home.

"Okay, Melania," Sarah's mom said. "Come out and end this if you can."

Sarah found herself holding her breath as she looked at her mom. She wasn't the only one—many of the potential combatants in the streets paused as the original Emerald Enchantress demonstrated what she could do if she was given room to work.

A thick mist filled the air. This by itself didn't do much to slow down the attackers, but it did give Dax and Keeley some cover to work with. They quickly scrambled out of the house, although Sarah wouldn't have been able to see them had it not been for the line of shadow creatures that burst into smoke as they took blows from Dax's sword or the number of them that suddenly clutched at their heads as Keeley's small but sharp claws slashed at their eyes and faces. As the mist spread, Sarah's mom continued to weave more spells.

A hissing noise ran through the air, starting as a whisper, getting louder until it sounded like the breathing of a giant snake, and then growing to a great roaring wind that blocked out all other sound. The space around her started to ripple and distort, changing color and shape as though her mom had turned the air around her into a multi-colored pool of water. Strange smells started to fill the area, sometimes even worse than the gremlins' stink-bombs but other times becoming as pleasant as fresh rose petals.

When Sarah breathed in through her mouth, she could even taste different things, ranging from fresh breads to copper coins to wet rocks. Each sensation only lasted seconds before changing to something else. At first, Sarah thought her mom was wasting energy, but then she saw that Melania's forces—and, more importantly, the innocent but brainwashed people of the Great City—were looking disoriented and woozy under the barrage of constant change.

Her mom was controlling their senses. If they couldn't rely on their hearing, sight, taste, or smell, they couldn't fight as effectively. Then she unleashed an attack on their sense of touch, showing them that the one thing they could reliably expect in the battle was pain.

The clouds darkened, and thunder boomed. The sky opened up with a frigid cold rain that chilled and stung. Then the rain turned to ice, sending hailstones and tiny frozen needles into the skin of Melania's forces. The hail struck with amazing precision. Even as Sarah, Kay, and Carrie found themselves surrounded by shadow-creatures, weather assaulted their enemies but left the children warm and dry.

Melania had sent her shadow-creatures in as the first wave. Those loyal to her within the Great City formed a ring around the battle but weren't able to get any closer due to the spells woven by Sarah's mom. Their enemy's tactics had backfired. While the shadow-things were no doubt better in a fight than typical merchants and farmers, they were also enemies that the companions didn't need to hold back against.

"Mom's made it easy," Sarah said to her friends. "Let's show her how thankful we are."

Sarah, Kay, and Carrie stood back-to-back and shoulder-to-shoulder, forming a tight ring from which they could launch their attacks. Carrie left the ring first, springing forward and stabbing with her blade. Her attacks were sloppy, but they struck home thanks to the distractions Sarah's mom had set up. Disoriented, the shadow people were forced to fight defensively, and they couldn't even see clearly to parry the attacks. The hailstones slapping against their skin probably hurt them more than the sword thrusts, but Carrie did her damage too.

Kay struck out with his staff, choosing to save his spells for a time when the inevitable backfire would be helpful rather than harmful. Sarah, on the other hand, had no such fears. Once again, she grinned at the ability to cut loose. This time, though, her common sense won out and informed her that she didn't need to rain down fire and brimstone. She just needed to take advantage of the rain her mom had already provided.

Fighting through the confusing haze brought on by her mom's spells, one of the shadow creatures lunged at Sarah with its claws outstretched. She easily dodged the clumsy blow. Then she noticed that in an attempt to stabilize itself, the creature had grabbed onto the shoulder of another shadow creature. Rather than send a lightning bolt through her attacker, Sarah scaled her spell back and just provided a little spark. The jolt of electricity ran through the wet creature, then into the other one he was touching. Both straightened out like they'd each stuck their tongues into light sockets. Then they dropped to the ground, unconscious.

"Okay," Sarah said, "maybe this whole restraint thing isn't always so bad after all."

The longer the battle went on, the more confident the companions got. Even though they were badly outnumbered, the tactical advantage was theirs. Slowly but surely, the number of shadow creatures dwindled. Unfortunately, Melania's first wave was only part of the battle.

Just as quickly as the creatures had appeared, they vanished. The world faded into blackness for a moment, and when light shined in the sky again, the creatures melted into wisps of smoke. The smoke all trailed to a common source, forming a woman with blonde hair and bright clothing but whose face was darkened with rage.

"That's Melania," Carrie said.

Unfortunately, the woman had appeared in the midst of another force—the throng of citizens of the Great City, who now waved clubs, knives, and even fists in defiance against the companions.

"What do we do now?" Sarah whispered to her companions. "I'm not going to zap people who don't deserve it."

"There's always sleep spells," Kay said. "And I'm sure Dax won't mind knocking them out instead of cutting them with his sword."

"But can we really take out a whole city?"

"Yes, we can," Sarah's mom said as she reached the companions' sides. Locking eyes with Melania, she raised her voice so everybody in the area could hear. "We can beat this whole city, but we're not interested in seeing others suffer. We're just here for you, Melania. Stop hiding behind innocents and face us. You can show us whether you really have the power it takes to rule, or I can do to these people what I did to your shadows. You don't want to be the ruler of an empty city, do you?"

Melania remained silent for a long time. Then she held up her hand. "Stand back, my loyal subjects."

The townsfolk looked almost as confused as the companions, but they obeyed Melania's command.

But rather than face the companions, the witch gave a long, shrill whistle. It seemed to echo for miles, and it was sharp enough that it felt like Sarah's eardrums were about to burst. When the whistle finally died away, the ground began to rumble.

"You're right, an army of peasants won't do much good against you. But let's see if you can beat my other champion."

The cobbled streets exploded in a spray of rock and dirt, sending Sarah's mom sprawling. Sarah would have rushed to help her, but she was paralyzed by the sight of the creature that had just burst out of the ground.

A shadow passed over the sun as the now-airborne dragon Grim-jaw soared above the companions. Sarah looked at her mom for guidance and saw a look of determination but not one of hope.

The storm clouds her mom had summoned hadn't cleared away yet, and at a word from her lips, they unleashed a burst of lightning that struck the dragon's scaly hide only to bounce off harmlessly.

Sarah ran toward her mom, and her friends followed.

"You've beaten a dragon before, right, Mom?"

"Yes, dear, I have."

"How did you do it?"

"I got lucky."

"Think you can repeat that?"

"She won't have to," a high-pitched voice said. "Keeley will stop cousin Grimjaw. You stop wicked Melania."

Without another word, the tiny dragon took to the air. She gave a mighty roar and spat a thick haze of smoke straight ahead. Flying into the cloud she'd just created, she seemed to vanish. Then she reappeared right next to Grimjaw's ear, snarling and growling something Sarah couldn't understand. Grimjaw growled back and tried to snap his giant fangs around tiny Keeley, but the small white dragon dodged out of the way. Then she spat a burst of flame directly into Grimjaw's face, causing the dragons to swerve in his flight. Grimjaw hit the side of a building, and a shower of wood and cracked stone rained down in the streets.

"Do you think she stands a chance?" Carrie asked.

"Do any of us stand a chance in the long run?" Dax queried.

Melania, for her part, looked more than a little nervous. Seeing a skilled swordsman and multiple spellcasters against her force of peasants seemed to shake her confidence. The fact that they were all willing to trust the smallest of their number to face their most deadly foe obviously left her wondering if Keeley was really that powerful or if they were all insane.

Sarah hoped it was the former. She certainly didn't want this to be her last stand.

Nineteen

"My mother used to tell me what to do when fighting a dragon," Dax said, eyeing the aerial battle that was unfolding between mighty Grimjaw and tiny Keeley.

"What did she say?" Sarah asked.

"Don't," Dax replied.

For a moment, Melania hesitated. Even with all the odds stacked in her favor, she seemed unwilling to believe she would win this fight. Then her eyes met with Carrie's, and an angry look took over her face.

"Attack," she told the citizens of the Great City. And they did.

Dozens—maybe even hundreds—of people in the town square rushed the companions, too many to hold back. The friends tried their best. Dax, Kay, and Carrie struck to disable and incapacitate rather than to kill. Sarah's mom threw about sleep spells as quickly as she could say the words, and Sarah herself blinded several of them with clouds of glittering golden dust. But all the spells in the world could only go so far.

Behind the men and women who fell, more people rushed in, all seemingly willing to die to protect Melania if they needed to. Soon, the companions were overrun. A large man with a butcher's knife tackled

Sarah and knocked her to the ground. Sarah's wand spun out of her grasp, and she found herself pinned under the heavy man's knees. He raised the knife and . . .

Nothing.

The man had Sarah at his mercy, but he hesitated. Unwilling to plunge a knife into a child even for his mistress Melania, he just let the weapon hover in his hand, a confused and conflicted look on his face.

Sarah took the opportunity to squirm out from under him and run. A quick glance told her that the other companions were finding the same thing—these citizens were willing to fight and hold the companions for Melania, but they didn't seem willing to deliver any sort of blow that would seriously wound them. This meant that disabling them without killing them was going to be much easier.

A crater opened up about a hundred feet away from the base of Melania's castle as Grimjaw landed hard. Keeley had focused her attacks on clawing the great dragon's eyes and ears, keeping him disoriented and always staying just out of reach. The larger dragon let out a roar of frustration, and Keeley took the opportunity to breathe fire down his throat, sending him into a coughing fit.

Amidst the confused throng of people and the dueling dragons, Melania began rushing toward the front gate of her palace.

"Oh no you don't," Sarah said. She started after her, but then the man with the knife grabbed her again. Sarah stomped her heel into his foot, causing him to scream and let her go. The momentary distraction gave Melania time to cast a spell of her own. She smiled and waved goodbye sarcastically as she disappeared in a puff of smoke which trailed back to the castle's shattered window.

"She's getting away!"

Sarah's shout alerted her mom, who managed to struggle free of two women who were trying to pull her down. She yelled the words to a paralysis spell, freezing a dozen people around her in place. Unfortunately, Grimjaw's rampage soon overshadowed such small victories.

The raging dragon finally managed to hit Keeley, swatting her with his long, bony tail when she tried to wheel around to the back of his head. She hit the ground, leaving a pothole-sized crater from the impact. Grimjaw followed up the attack with a long burst of fire. When the flames cleared, Keeley was left ash-gray and barely moving.

Carrie was the first to break away from her attackers to come to the dragon's rescue, but she ran blindly into battle, ignoring the obvious danger. A swipe of Grimjaw's claw would have taken her head off had Kay not caught up with her at the last moment and thrown himself on top of her, pulling both of them to the ground. Without getting up, Kay rolled over and launched a ray of fire from the tip of his staff. Much to Sarah's surprise, the spell seemed to work exactly as intended. Much to her dismay, it didn't do anything other than leave a small black spot on the dragon's hide.

"Magic and dragons don't mix, boy!" Grimjaw shouted. "We're older than most spells and more deadly than most fire. Your spells can't even slow me down."

The dragon roared and beat his wings, creating enough wind to knock the hat off Kay's head. The only good news from the situation seemed to be that with Melania now out of sight and a terrifying dragon in the streets, the cityfolk had regained enough of their senses to run the other way rather than continue to attack the companions.

"Let's test those words, shall we?" Sarah's mom called. Bursts of dirt and rubble shot out from the ground in a dozen different places, surrounding Grimjaw. From each of those spots came a large humanoid figure almost ten feet tall, created out of the rocks themselves. Sarah recognized them from her spellbook—golems. They were magical protectors, hopefully strong enough to put a dent in a dragon's hide.

"Ha-ha!" the dragon cried, more amused than threatened. "I haven't had a workout like this in at least fifty years!"

The golems grappled with Grimjaw, grabbing his wings so he couldn't fly and pulling him to the ground while they pummeled him with fists of stone. For a moment, they seemed to overpower the beast. Then a cracking sound tore through the air, and the dragon fought back. Rocks flew through the sky like dirt in the wind as one of the golems' arms broke. Grimjaw rolled on top of another, then turned over entirely and got back to his feet. He struck out with claws, wings, and tail, literally breaking his foes wherever he hit them. Then he grabbed the last one in his jaw, crunching it into rubble like it was nothing more than stale bread.

Sarah took half a second to survey the scene. Dax was battling the few stragglers who remained following Melania's retreat and Grimjaw's arrival. Carrie crouched over Keeley, trying to protect the wounded dragon from the surrounding chaos. Kay was preparing a spell, and Sarah didn't worry about how it might backfire. It wasn't like he could make things worse.

A swarm of purple and yellow butterflies flew from Kay's staff. They engulfed Grimjaw like a multicolored cloud. Unfazed, Grimjaw laughed loudly.

"Boy, I've never seen a less competent wizard."

In response, Kay clenched his fist. The colored cloud around Grimjaw suddenly lit up in flame. Each butterfly made a loud popping noise and exploded against the dragon's hide, as though the butterflies had turned into a massive string of firecrackers that all exploded at once.

It was a spell Sarah had never read about or even imagined before. Even in the midst of battle, she felt a surge of pride for her friend. Reliable or not, his spells were definitely getting impressive.

"I need to get him a notebook of some sort," Sarah murmured. "He should start writing those spells down."

While Grimjaw burned, Sarah rushed to her mom's side. The two enchantresses both unleashed flames of their own, creating an inferno. She figured nothing could survive that kind of heat . . .until Grimjaw proved her wrong.

The dragon's skin glowed like burning embers, but that didn't seem to do much more than make him angry. Sarah's mom summoned up a crystalline shield, which only barely turned aside Grimjaw's claws. Kay prepared another spell, but a swipe of the dragon's tail ended the casting. Carrie yelled in panic as the boy hit the ground. Sarah was just happy to see that her friend's head was still on his shoulders after taking the blow.

She thought of an offensive spell but realized her mom's defenses wouldn't hold under the dragon's assault. She channeled her magical energy into helping to support her mom's shield instead. This only bought them another second or two. With another mighty blow, Grimjaw shattered both their spells and left them defenseless.

Crystal shards pelted them, raining down upon them like needles from the sky. As much as the tiny splinters of crystal hurt, the looming dragon's claws meant something much worse. Sarah's first instinct was to protect her mom. Unfortunately, her mom's first instinct was to protect her daughter. The two collided in an awkward diving hug, trying to pull each other to the ground and serve as a mutual human shield.

As a result, both of them suffered at the hands of the dragon. Grimjaw's claw raked against Sarah's mom's back, cutting deeply enough to draw a scream and some blood. Sarah seemed to escape unscathed, but then the dragon's swipe broke some of the ground near her. A chunk of rock the size of a large dog flew up and landed on her leg, twisting her ankle painfully and leaving her trapped underneath its weight.

"You wizards," Grimjaw growled. "You always assume that magic will solve your problems. I'd let you call this a lesson learned, but Melania doesn't care anymore whether you live or die. I prefer the latter."

Hundreds of curved yellow teeth loomed overhead as Grimjaw prepared to swallow the enchantresses whole. Sarah felt sick as she realized that her current adventure in Greystone Valley was almost certainly going to be her last.

Twenty

Sarah closed her eyes, waiting for the inevitable. Then she heard something that seemed out of place on the battlefield: the sound of one old man clearing his throat repeatedly.

"Ahem. A-herm-herm-harrum." Dax was covered in dirt, sweat, and grime but still looked better off than any of the companions. He stepped over a pile of unconscious foes and began to advance upon the dragon.

"It's like my mother always warned me: when it comes to fighting dragons, don't. But if you absolutely have to, win."

The market square of the Great City lay in absolute ruins, with crumbled buildings, craters in the street, and everything but Melania's palace bearing scorch marks. Dax looked like a small, gray speck wandering across a wasteland.

"I've broken the spells of your wizards," Grimjaw said. "Do you really think you can beat me, old man?"

"Almost certainly not," Dax said. "But if there must be a fight to the death, the first person to lose might as well be poor old Dax."

"Dax, eh? That will be an awfully short name to put on your tombstone."

"Daxilianus Pouranger Asilas the Third," the old warrior corrected him. "The thirteenth son of the thirteenth son. The lonely warrior of the forgotten realm. But don't worry, the advantage is still yours. It's been years since I slew a dragon."

Unimpressed, Grimjaw shot a jet of flame from his nostrils. Dax, however, began to move as soon as he saw the dragon inhale. Taking advantage of the rubble around the battlefield, he dove behind a collapsed stone wall and used it as a shield against the fire. When the flames died down, Dax emerged from behind his cover with some ash smeared on his face and a few strands of hair singed away but otherwise none the worse for wear.

The old warrior started running, and the dragon met his charge. The earth shook as Grimjaw sped across the ground much faster than anything that big had a right to move. Grimjaw seemed about to snap Dax up in his jaws, but the warrior went into a slide at the last possible second. The dragon's teeth closed on empty air, and Dax raked his sword against the monster's gullet.

Grimjaw roared and slammed his front claws against the ground, but Dax was already on his feet again and moving fast. As the ground buckled in on itself like a rocky tsunami, the warrior rushed along with perfect balance, slashing at the dragon wherever he could get close. By the time Grimjaw reared up on his back feet, he had a half-dozen bleeding wounds. Again and again the warrior struck, each time averting his eyes just as his sword landed and then moving on before he had a chance to see the blood he was drawing from his foe.

"You stupid swordsman!" Grimjaw yelled in rage. "This is nothing! You're just a flea! And you will—ow!"

Dax jammed his blade all the way to the hilt in the space between two claws on Grimjaw's back foot, demonstrating that this flea could bite.

For a moment, Sarah found herself mesmerized by her companion's deft movements. She'd seen him in battle before and trusted that he could hold his own against almost anything, but he was fighting on a whole other level now. She'd never seen him move so quickly or fight so desperately. A moment ago, Sarah figured that it would take a miracle to save her and her mom from winding up in Grimjaw's belly. Now, Dax was in the process of delivering that miracle.

She finally broke away from watching the battle and tried to pry herself free of the rubble which had pinned her to the ground. Other than a nasty twist in her ankle, she thought she was fine. If anything was broken, surely there would have been more pain by now. All she needed was to get the meddlesome stone off of her so she could get back in the fight. But she couldn't move it.

Sarah's mom didn't seem to be in much shape to help thanks to the wound that now ran along the length of her back. She tried to focus her magical talent to help Dax, but her spell turned into nothing more than some green smoke as her mind failed to cut through the haze of pain she was in. She then tried to help Sarah with the rock, but attempting to lift it only opened the wound wider. With a cry of pain, she fell down again. Sarah took her mom's hand, squeezing it and silently urging her not to try to get up.

"Let's see how well you fly!" Grimjaw yelled when he realized that Dax was starting to cause him serious pain on the ground. The dragon leapt up and took to the air, but the warrior wasn't about to let his foe get away that easily. Sinking his blade into Grimjaw's leg, Dax let his foe take him into the sky. Once he got a grip on one of the dragon's spines, he pulled his sword free and climbed carefully up the beast's back. Grimjaw did a barrel roll and loop-de-loop in the air, trying to shake Dax free, but the old warrior held on like his life depended on it, which, at that altitude, it almost certainly did.

Even as she watched Dax climb along the dragon's back, Sarah swore she could hear him moaning about how badly his arthritis was going to bother him in the morning.

Back on the ground, the companions had regrouped—sort of. Carrie held Keeley in one hand as though she were carrying an egg and let a semi-conscious Kay lean on her as they staggered over to Sarah and her mom. Once they got there, Kay dropped to his hands and knees. Their best hope now was Dax.

Grimjaw had been flailing about in the air as though trying to scratch an itch he couldn't quite reach. One of his wild swings managed to strike true, leaving massive claw marks along Dax's side that drew a yell of pain from the warrior. Dax responded by driving his sword repeatedly into the muscle at the base of the dragon's wing. Grimjaw spat a fireball into the sky before the sword strokes did their work and left him unable to keep flying. Both dragon and warrior plummeted to the ground at the far end of the market square, but only one of them was properly equipped for a crash landing.

Grimjaw hit the street head-first and slid along the ground like a massive boat that had just collided with the shore. The impact finally jarred Dax loose. Although he managed to keep a grip on his sword, he didn't protect himself well from the impending crash. The old man hit the ground and slid along like a pebble somebody had just kicked down a hill. The only thing that stopped him was the side of a stone building. He hit that hard enough that Sarah swore she heard the cracking of bone more than a hundred feet away. She found herself holding her breath, terrified that Dax wasn't going to get up.

He did rise, but he did so slowly. His right arm raised his sword again. His left arm dangled useless at his side, broken in the fall.

"Carrie, help get this stone off me!" Sarah shouted. "Hurry!"

Carrie set Keeley down next to the recovering Kay. Then both she and Sarah's mom struggled to lift the rock. Neither of them had the strength left to move it much, but they managed to shift it enough that Sarah could get free. She pulled herself to her feet and half-ran, half-limped in Dax's direction.

Grimjaw, too, was on the move again. He charged Dax on all fours. Too angry for words, the dragon had nothing but an earth-shaking bellow to offer as he prepared to end the battle. One wing flapped wildly as Grimjaw ran. The other stuck out at an odd angle, useless thanks to the warrior's sword.

Dax stood his ground as the dragon bore down on him. Sarah was reminded of a bull-fighter, but this one didn't have a red cape and a cheering crowd. Instead, he waited for the dragon with the same grimness with which he approached every task.

Just as Grimjaw was about to bite down on Dax's soft flesh, the warrior spun out of the way with so much grace and speed that Sarah forgot he was injured. He slashed high with his blade, cutting above Grimjaw's right eye and almost blinding his foe. His speed didn't save him entirely, though. One of the dragon's claws sliced across the back of his thigh. With a gasp and a stumble, Dax dropped to one knee.

That moment of weakness was all the dragon needed. Grimjaw turned quickly and snapped his teeth around Dax. Sarah screamed in panic as she saw the warrior disappear into the beast's mouth.

She called out the words to the first spell she could think of. Waving her hands, she sent rocks and debris from across the battlefield flying through the air, pummeling Grimjaw with anything she could find. Her mom flew into a similar rage, summoning up more golems to assault the monster. Carrie, Kay, and the newly awakened Keeley all rushed at Grimjaw, not even considering the fact that none of them were as effective as Dax himself.

Grimjaw coughed and gagged as the old warrior proved to be tougher to swallow than he'd though. When he opened his jaws, Dax was standing inside, badly wounded but still frantically driving his sword into the roof of his enemy's mouth in an attempt to strike the monster's brain. Grimjaw threw himself to the ground and rolled wildly. He flew into a frenzy as he experienced a sensation that dragons rarely felt in their lifetimes: fear.

One last burst of flame came from the dragon's jaws, but the fire died quickly. Sarah had closed to only a few dozen feet now. Over the sound of the golems mercilessly pounding on the monster's hide, she heard a crack and a squishing noise from inside the dragon's mouth where Dax had been stabbing ruthlessly. Grimjaw gave a groan, then fell face down on the ground. He didn't get up.

The golems disappeared, crumbling back into the earth from which they'd sprung. The spellfire and smoke died away. Then, from out of the dragon's half-open jaw, a single figure emerged. Dax was battered and burned, but he was victorious.

"I think . . . this is going to hurt . . . in the morning."

Dax took a few steps, then his legs gave out. He dropped his sword and collapsed a few feet from where the slain dragon lay.

Sarah was the first to reach him. When she got close to him, she almost felt her heart stop. Close up, wounds that had looked superficial ran much deeper. Sarah rolled Dax over onto his back and found that he was struggling just to breathe.

When Sarah spoke, it didn't seem like her own voice. She sounded like a frightened child who'd just had a bad dream.

"Dax . . . say something."

The old man's eyes stared off into the distance. Then, with great effort, he focused on Sarah's face.

"Are you okay?" he asked.

"Yes," she said, sounding more like herself now. "I'm going to be fine."

"And your mother? And the others?"

"She's fine too. We're all okay. You saved us all."

Dax closed his eyes. "Good. Then I think . . . I'm happy."

He smiled.

Then he died.

Twenty-One

On the worst day of her life, Sarah told herself that at least she would never hurt like that again. She never realized she could be wrong.

Sarah, there's been an accident.

The others joined her. Each of the humans dropped to their knees and touched Dax's unmoving body. Keeley climbed on top of the warrior and nudged his chin with her head as though she were trying to wake him up.

An accident . . .

She didn't cry. She hadn't cried then either. Crying would have meant there was something inside her, and she was empty through and through.

Sarah, there's been . . .

And then she was eleven years old again, falling asleep on the couch and waiting for her dad to come home. She woke up in the morning to see the bright rays of sunshine coming through the window, and her dad still wasn't there.

. . . an accident.

Everybody called it an accident. Even she referred to it that way from time to time. But it had never really felt like an accident. Somebody had taken her dad away from her. Accidents could be forgiven.

She'd never met the man who took her father away. He was sitting in a jail cell somewhere, a faceless killer she could only imagine. But even though the aching sense of loss was familiar, this situation was different. She knew who had taken Dax away. Grimjaw had been the weapon, but the real killer had a name and a face Sarah could recognize. And nobody would ever call what Melania had done an accident. She had to be stopped.

"I . . . I didn't really know him very well," Carrie said with a touch of guilt in her voice.

"None of us knew him well enough," Kay replied. "He didn't really talk about himself, unless it was to complain. He was probably the most miserable man I've ever met." He shook his head. "Poor old Dax," he said, nearly choking on the words.

"Keeley is sorry," whispered the white dragon to the fallen warrior. "She promised to protect her friends. Dragons are always supposed to keep their word." She looked at Melania's palace, and the tip of her snout trembled. "But now, Keeley makes another promise. She promises that the evil witch will never hurt anybody again!"

She punctuated this oath with a roar, then took to the air, flying straight toward the broken window at the front of the palace.

"Keeley, wait!" Sarah's mom called. "We need to regroup!"

But the dragon didn't listen. Neither did Sarah, who gripped her wand tightly and ran as fast as her aching legs would carry her toward the castle's front gate. Her mom sighed and rushed after them, determined to make sure that nobody else shared Dax's fate.

Keeley launched herself through the hole in the window, and the inside of the castle immediately started to burn. Not having wings, the rest of the companions had to go through the front door. It was locked, but

Sarah was only too happy to blast the gate open with a spell. With a wave of her wand, she lifted a chunk of rock that had once been part of a building and used it as a battering ram.

Sarah was the first to charge through the shattered entryway. She fell immediately into shadow.

What had appeared to be the grand entrance hallway of a royal palace dissolved into inky darkness. The floor underneath Sarah's feet gave way, and she tumbled, but she didn't fall very far. She was suddenly weightless, floating in nothingness like she was a spirit. No light, no direction. Then from out of nowhere came Melania's voice.

"You want me to be the villain of this story, but I'm not," it said, echoing through miles of black shadow. "I had brought order and happiness to this world. Your friends cared more about being heroes than doing what was best for everybody. As for you . . . if you had just stayed in your world and forgotten about this one, that old man would still be alive."

Sarah gritted her teeth and flailed her arms and legs in an attempt to fight through the shadow. She moved forward slowly as though she were swimming through gelatin.

"Why are you still fighting?" Melania asked. "If you keep attacking me, you're only going to get more people killed. They'll all die, and it will be your fault."

The words seemed meant to stop her, to make her wallow in guilt and grief. But Sarah had already been through all that. For days and weeks after her dad was taken from her, she kept blaming herself. Hadn't she felt a little sick that morning? If she had complained about her stomach more, maybe her dad would have stayed home to take care of her instead of leaving. What if she had called him at work before he got into the car? Telling him how much she loved him just once more might have stopped him from being in the wrong place at the wrong time.

Melania wanted her to feel guilt. Sarah had lived with guilt for years.

"We don't have to fight," Melania said. "I can make you forget the pain. I can bring Dax back to you. I can make all of your wishes come true."

Sarah pushed harder.

Melania's voice rose in frustration. "Why do you still resist?"

"Because I don't want to forget, and you can't give back what you took away," Sarah hissed.

With one last burst of effort, she discovered she hadn't been pushing against anything at all. She was still on the first floor of the palace, looking at the red carpet that ran up the stairs. Battle raged all around her as the remainder of Melania's shadow creatures faced off against her friends. A portion of the balcony up above had been burned to embers by Keeley's flame. A crackle of lightning burst from her mom's wand. Carrie and Kay stood back to back, wielding sword and staff to ward off their assailants.

"Good!" Carrie shouted. "You're back!"

Her eyes drifted upward. Keeley darted to and fro, tearing at ears and noses with her claws and teeth. Amidst all the chaos stood Melania, seemingly ignored by the rest of the companions. Her eyes met with Sarah's. Then she started running.

"Why are you dealing with the minions instead of their leader?" Sarah shouted.

"If we could find her, we'd deal with her!" Kay called.

Wondering how they could miss Melania, Sarah charged up the stairs alone.

"Wait for us!" Carrie shouted. The rest of the companions moved to follow, but the shadow creatures closed ranks around them, creating a wall of opponents that prevented them from following Sarah.

Sarah didn't slow her charge. Her mind burning with rage, all she could think about was finding Melania and making her pay.

Leaving the field of battle, she rushed through the castle corridors, hot on her enemy's heels. Doors closed just in front of her, and she threw them open without thinking about what might be waiting on the other side. At some of the bends, she feared she was about to lose the witch. At other times, she seemed close enough to reach out and grab her. After a long minute of the frustrating chase, she finally burst through a door and found Melania waiting for her with nowhere left to run.

The chamber looked like a throne room, with tall pillars supporting a domed roof and comfortable chairs lining the walls. At the center of the room was a large throne carved out of what looked like white wood. Taking another look at it, Sarah realized that it was bone.

"When Greystone Valley had a king, this was the place where he was crowned," Melania said, circling the throne. She held her hands up as though she were ready to cast a spell. Sarah tracked her with her wand, ready to blast the villain if she tried anything. "What if I were to give all this up right now? I could give you the throne and use my powers to make you a queen. Would you be a good ruler, Sarah?"

Sarah shook her head. "I don't want to rule. I'm still just a kid."

"Then why do the people of this land rely on you so much? Why would your mother let her own child into a world like this?"

"She trusts me."

"Trust." Melania turned the word over in her mouth as though she had never used it before. "Friendship. Those are just words. They're things people say to make it seem like somebody else in this world—in any world—cares about them. I've spent my life trying to find those things, and I can tell you right now that those words are as fake as the illusions I create."

"You're a liar and a coward," Sarah said.

"Then why is a teenage girl facing off against the conqueror of Greystone Valley all by herself?"

It was only then that Sarah realized what Kay had tried to tell her. "Because they didn't see you."

Her stomach sank as she realized she'd probably run right into another trap. But she recovered quickly.

"The others will be along any minute now," she said, more to calm herself down than to intimidate Melania. "But by then, I'll have already dealt with you."

Melania's ruby lips drew into a vicious smile. "That confident, are you? Very well . . . show me what you've got."

Twenty-Two

Carrie didn't land many blows in the battle, but she did get the last one. A lunge from her blade pierced the shadow-creature's chest, and it melted away into nothingness.

"They're getting weaker," she said to her companions. "Melania's monsters used to be like flesh and blood human beings, but now they're just smoke, disappearing whenever we hit them. Why do you think that is?"

"Maybe Melania's getting weaker," Kay said hopefully.

"No, she just had her attention focused somewhere else." Keeley flapped down from the balcony up above and landed on Carrie's shoulder. "Sarah didn't stay to fight," the tiny dragon yelped. "Keeley watched her run right past the shadow-men and down the hall!"

"We saw it from down here too," Sarah's mom chimed in. "And what's more, none of Melania's minions attacked her as she ran past them. She must have seen something we didn't."

Carrie cast her eyes up the long flight of stairs leading higher into the castle. Looking at the broken glass on the next floor, she now recognized the green-clad enchantress as the woman standing right next to her. Still, that wasn't the first thing on her mind right now.

"Ugh . . . wasn't I trying to get out of here not too long ago?"

"That was before we had our change of plans," Kay said.

"So what's the next part of our plan?" Carrie asked.

A burst of sound from several floors above shook the entire palace. Some plaster came off the ceiling and landed in front of Carrie's feet.

"Catching up to Sarah . . . and hopefully doing so before she brings the entire building down on top of us. Whatever's going on upstairs, I bet she could use our help."

A bolt of lightning shot out from Sarah's wand, but it went right through Melania.

"When I was young, I used my magic like you do now." Melania disappeared as she finished the sentence, then reappeared behind Sarah. "Force only went so far . . . especially in a world where they feared what my magic could do."

Sarah responded by giving her a taste of fire. Again, the attack went right through her. The witch disappeared, reappearing on the bone throne. Sarah didn't cast another spell this time. She knew by now that Melania wasn't really where she seemed to be.

"I don't know if I could shoot lightning or fire now if I tried," Melania said. "Eventually, I learned that the real power lies in controlling people's perceptions."

She waved a hand, and the throne room disappeared. Sarah and Melania were now in a forest, with the trees bare and leaves of orange, red, and brown forming a carpet on the ground. The air felt cold and damp, and Sarah could even smell the wet bark and decaying leaves around her. Only the bone throne remained, now seeming very out of place in the middle of a forest. Melania stood up and started walking, leaves crunching underneath her feet.

"We're not really here, of course," she said. "But it certainly seems that way, doesn't it? I daresay that you wouldn't even be able to find the way out of this room if you tried. And your friends won't be able to find you, because I've blocked the door with the illusion of a wall. All it took to isolate you from the others was a bit of shadow and a few whispered words. For all the magical might you've shown, you simply don't have that kind of power."

Sarah looked into the gray sky that she knew wasn't really there. There was something missing. She thought of Keeley and realized what it was: there were no birds, squirrels, or other small animals. Melania could paint an interesting picture with her illusions, but she couldn't make that world completely real.

"Power?" Sarah asked. "If you have so much power, why were you so afraid of me?"

"Who said I was afraid of you?"

"You erased people's memories so my mom and I wouldn't come to this world. You kidnapped Carrie, thinking she was me. And you tore your own city apart trying to stop me before I faced you."

Melania smiled the type of smile a person gave when they'd just told a joke that only they understood. "That is your perception."

The words made Sarah pause, but only for a moment. What was Melania's true plan? She'd assumed it was a simple matter of conquest. Given the chance, who wouldn't want to rule a land? Hadn't that been the type of threat Greystone Valley had faced before?

But what if there was something more? For the first time in what seemed to be forever, Sarah wished her mom was here—not to give her emotional support or comfort, but for actual advice that she could listen to. Her mom had been trying to slow down and think of a plan from the beginning. But time and again, Sarah had rushed ahead without thinking of what would happen next. Now she faced a witch who might be just as powerful as she was, and she had no friends to help her.

The good thing about jumping into situations like this headfirst was that now Sarah had no choice but to act. Whether she knew everything about Melania or not, she had a chance to stop her . . . if she could find her.

"What do you want?" Sarah asked, trying to buy some time.

"I want what you have," Melania replied. "But don't read too much into that. What I want has changed constantly since I've been in this valley. At first, I thought I could bring the sense of peace and order that the land needed."

The forest scene disappeared, and Sarah found herself in the sunlit streets of the Great City. People milled about, some walking right through Melania as they went on with their lives. Up above, the tall clock tower ticked with steady, perfect consistency.

"I gave these people everything they wanted. They had no reason not to feel content every second of every day. But what good is that when they couldn't give me what I wanted? Time and time again, I invited guests into my tower, but I couldn't very well hold a conversation with somebody whose mind was that addled. And when I released them from my spell—just to hold a conversation, mind you . . ." Her face darkened, and the world changed again. This time, Sarah found herself high in some isolated mountains, ankle deep in snow and shivering with cold. " . . . they thought I was a monster. They screamed and panicked, so I had to silence them. I never even got a word of thanks."

The mountains rumbled slightly. The sun grew dim, and from the cold shadowy air materialized the black-clad clawed men that served as Melania's minions. Four of them appeared in all, each standing a few feet behind Sarah, ready to strike should Melania ask.

"When your friends left through Castle Greystone to find you, I thought I should be afraid. I struck at you first through my shadows, but they're not always easy to control. I made a mistake. And then I found something very unusual. Carrie had no reason to pretend to be a sorceress. If she had just told me the truth, I would have erased her memory of this world and let her go. But she kept up with her charade even after I was almost certain she wasn't the one I wanted. So what do I want? I want to know who you are, Sarah. What's so special about you that a frightened girl who has no business being on an adventure is willing to put herself through pain and peril if she thinks it might protect you? What makes people willing to travel to other worlds to find you? I want to know the answer to that, and I want that power for myself."

Melania paced from side to side as she spoke, gesturing wildly with her hands as she became more excited. All the while, Sarah watched her feet. They left no footprints in the snow. The Melania who was speaking wasn't really there, but the real one must have been close by. If she could find some way to break through the illusion . . .

"What makes you think it's something special about me? Maybe my friends are all just crazy."

The shadow creatures each placed a hand on their swords. "Don't make the mistake of thinking I'm stupid. There's something about you that gives you power over them."

Now it was Sarah's turn to smile. "That is your perception."

As quickly as she could, she whispered the words to a spell. A magical wind whipped through the mountains, or rather the throne room that Melania had made look like mountains. Snow flew in every direction, passing through the illusory Melania and pelting her shadow creatures with white powder. As the mini-whirlwind blew around them, Sarah watched carefully for that which didn't belong. Her patience was rewarded when she saw a break in the flurrying snow—a human-shaped outline that had previously been invisible.

"Gotcha," Sarah muttered. *"Nivus no ceo."*

Shards of ice flew from Sarah's wand, pelting the invisible figure with a magical barrage. With a shout, the previously invisible Melania appeared, and the snowy illusion vanished. The shadow creatures, however, did not.

Melania touched a spot on her cheek where one of Sarah's ice shards had struck. She pulled her hand away, saw the red smear of blood, and glared at her opponent.

"What was that you were saying about your illusions being more powerful than my magic?" Sarah asked confidently.

"You tell me," Melania retorted. "I still have you outnumbered."

The four shadow creatures charged, their swords drawn and claws bared. With a wave of her wand and the call of a few magic words, Sarah made the whole palace shift and shudder. The domed ceiling high above her began to crack. One of the pillars broke. Before the stones hit the ground, Sarah called to them with another spell. The rubble flew at her enemies, pelting the shadow creatures with sharp shards and heavy debris. The creatures fell to the ground, then disappeared in a puff of smoke.

Sarah took a deep breath, trying not to show that the last spell had set her heart pounding like a jackhammer. Her friends were still in the castle—the last thing she needed to do was bring the whole building down on top of them.

Giving in to frustration, Melania charged at Sarah, trying to attack her with bare hands. That loss of composure got Sarah to refocus on the battle. She waved her wand like she was conducting a magical orchestra. A large chunk of stone flew toward Melania, striking her in the stomach and knocking her flat on her back. The force caused her to slide across the floor, ultimately coming to a stop a few feet away from the bone throne.

Sarah pointed her wand at her foe before the witch could get up. Seeing no room for escape, Melania slumped and stayed still.

"You really are the person I've been looking for." She almost sounded like she admired Sarah.

Footsteps approached the chamber. "This way!" Kay's voice said. "A door just appeared!"

"You're done now," Sarah said.

"Hardly," Melania said. "I have exactly what I want."

She snapped her fingers, and everything suddenly changed. A wave of dizziness overtook Sarah, and her body started to ache. Her vision blurred, and her mouth tasted as though she'd been sucking on pennies. Despite the disorientation, she kept her wand trained on Melania. But then she realized something very strange: she had no wand at all. And Melania had disappeared.

When Sarah looked at the person lying in front of the floor, she saw herself.

But that didn't make any sense. She was still standing, a finger pointed at her foe instead of a wand. Then she realized that the finger didn't belong to her. It was long and slender with a well-manicured nail. Instead of her green robes, she wore a rust-colored blouse. Just a moment ago, Melania had worn those same clothes.

"What just happened?" she asked. But she wasn't really the one speaking. Realization dawned on her as she heard Melania's voice come out of her mouth.

"Perception is more powerful than reality," the person who now wore Sarah's face said. She glanced at the door as the rest of the companions began banging against it. "You'll see."

The door flew open. Kay was the first through. He didn't stop to ask questions. To his eyes, it looked like Melania was standing over a helpless Sarah, ready to deal the final blow. He acted instantly. The spell that came out of his mouth was one Sarah didn't recognize. He thrust his staff forward, and a black ray shot at her. It struck the person he thought was his enemy, and Sarah felt every part of her body light up like she was on fire. She screamed in pain, then watched in horror as pieces of her body vanished. She felt herself burn away into black ash.

In less than a second, the pain ended . . . and Sarah was gone.

Twenty-Three

nly a burned spot on the ground marked where Melania had been. The threat was over, but Carrie still felt sick to her stomach.

Kay shook from head to toe after casting the spell. He dropped his staff and looked like he might fall over. Sarah, who had been lying on the ground at Melania's mercy, jumped to her feet and rushed toward Kay, giving him a long hug.

"You saved me," she said.

His face pale, Kay nodded. He seemed to have nothing to say. His eyes remained locked on the space where Melania had been.

"I've never seen something like that before," Sarah's mom said. "What kind of spell did you cast?"

"She's . . . she's gone," Kay said. "Sometimes, my spells get away from me, but this time, I was so focused. I was just so angry about Dax, and when I saw Sarah in trouble, I knew I had to do something. I . . ." The look of shock vanished, replaced by a grim expression, as though Kay had just grown up in an instant. "She'll never hurt anybody else."

Sarah's mom turned toward her daughter. "Why did you run ahead like that? You could have gotten yourself killed."

Carrie expected Sarah to snap back at her mom, but instead, she looked like she was about to burst into tears.

"I'm sorry," she said, letting Kay go and throwing her arms around her mom. "I've learned my lesson. I won't go it alone ever again."

"It . . . it's okay, sweetie," a surprised mother said. "It all worked out in the end."

"Yes, yes it did!" Keeley shouted, flying circles near the top of the massive throne room. "Keeley will tell the dragons the great tale of how her friends fought through the illusions of the evil enchantress! Tales will be sung of brave Sarah—both versions of them—and all the rest of us who helped free Greystone Valley! And Dax . . ." The dragon landed on Carrie's shoulder and bowed her head respectfully. "Dax will be remembered most of all."

"What about the people outside?" Carrie asked. "Will they still be affected by Melania's memory charms?"

"No," Sarah said. "I, uh, don't think they will. With the evil witch gone, there's no reason her spells would last, is there? But I guess there's only one way to find out."

She tugged at her mom's sleeve with one hand and grabbed Kay by the arm with her other. She led the two out of the throne room and toward the palace's exit. Carrie followed with Keeley on her shoulder, but she looked back at the burned mark on the floor and couldn't help but feel that something was very wrong.

That night, Carrie became a hero by association. While she'd used what Dax had taught her in the fight against Melania's forces, she wasn't an expert swordswoman. She didn't fly or breathe fire, and she certainly couldn't cast spells. But the people of the Great City included her in the celebration nonetheless, mostly because she'd been lucky enough to be friends with the people who had really saved the day.

At least that's how she felt. Her new friends seemed to think she played a bigger role in Melania's defeat.

"Keeley thought you were very impressive," the tiny dragon said into her ear. "You fought bravely and helped save us when cousin Grimjaw attacked!"

"She's right," Kay said. "Most people probably would have curled up in a ball and cried when they were captured by Melania. You should hold your head high."

With that encouragement, that's exactly what Carrie did. There was a moment of initial confusion when they emerged from the palace, but the locals quickly recovered and hailed them as the saviors of the Great City. Although Sarah and her mom got most of the attention—after all, everybody now remembered the legendary Emerald Enchantresses—the rest of the companions all got their due as well. Kay was Greystone Valley's native son, Keeley was the fire-breathing dragon of the northern mountains, and most people referred to Carrie as the swordmaiden trained by Dax himself. She didn't correct them by telling them that her training had only been a few hours at the most. Now that Dax had fallen in the defense of the city, many of the people seemed determined to see him as one of Greystone Valley's greatest heroes—which he was, as far as any of the companions were concerned—and many people seemed to take comfort in the idea that his legacy lived on in Carrie.

By nightfall, the Great City had transformed from a battle zone into a celebration the likes of which Carrie had never seen. Fireworks burst in the sky, speeches were given, and people cheered in the streets wherever the companions went. The only break from the celebration was the long moment of silence as Dax received a hero's burial. Fine food was served, as was strong wine—wine which Sarah's mom kept her daughter from drinking and which Carrie knew better than to try after her experience in Melania's tower.

As the celebrations died down, the companions were given a suite of rooms in the finest inn in the city. Carrie took their word for it when it came to the quality—a medieval inn certainly didn't have the swimming pool, waffle maker, or television she was used to when her family stayed at a hotel.

"It seems strange that everybody's so happy," Sarah said, speaking to Carrie for the first time since the confusion of the festival began. "I mean, they were enchanted, not slaves."

"They were only allowed to feel what Melania told them to feel," Carrie replied. "That's practically the definition of slavery."

Sarah crooked an eyebrow. "Well, I guess we should all be glad she's gone for good, shouldn't we?"

The suite had a common area with a fireplace, a single glass window that gave a wonderful view of the clock tower, and several comfortable chairs with soft feather pillows to help cushion them. Despite these luxuries, Sarah and Carrie sat cross-legged on the floor while Sarah's mom and Kay took the chairs. Keeley spent her time alternating which companion sported her as a headpiece. Right now, she was on Sarah's mom, whipping the enchantress's dark hair back and forth with her tail.

"Is this what you wanted, Kay?" Sarah asked. "Not very long ago, you were on the run from a warlord. Now you've slain the evil mindwitch or whatever silly title they'll give her in the history books."

Kay stared at the tip of his staff thoughtfully. He didn't seem happy, and he didn't seem sad. He just seemed . . . distant.

"I usually love magic," he said quietly. "Sometimes, I get reminded that even good wizards can't always stay away from the darker side of it."

"If you ever need somebody to talk to—" Sarah's mom began.

Kay smiled sheepishly. "Oh, I know I can come to you. After all, you've got more stories told about you than anybody else in this room put together. I'm sure those tales left out their share of unhappy moments too."

Sarah's mom nodded. Keeley stopped playing with her hair and took to the air, finding a new perch on Sarah's shoulder.

Sarah twitched in an uncomfortable way, as though she were unfamiliar with having the tiny dragon land on her. Keeley gave her a quizzical look, then hopped over to Carrie instead.

Outside, the clock rang eleven times.

Sarah stood up and stretched. "Magical land aside, I still have a bedtime, right, Mom?"

"I think that's the first time you haven't fought me on it in years."

"Funny how nearly getting killed by an evil sorceress tends to change things," Sarah quipped. Then she became more serious, and her eyes grew pleading. "No offense to anybody here, but I just want to go home for a while and live a normal life, okay?"

Sarah's mom nodded. "Darling, sometimes the best part of an adventure is when it ends. We'll return to Castle Greystone in the morning and then spend some time picking up our lives where we left off." She got up and nodded to each of the people remaining in the room. "Good night, everybody."

Then, Sarah and her mom entered one of the suite's three bedrooms to get some sleep.

"Are you sure we can't just use a spell to travel to the castle tonight?" Carrie asked. "My family's probably worried sick about me."

"Don't worry about it," Kay said. "Time tends to run pretty closely both here and there, but it's not exact. You may have spent a few days here, but in your world, only a few hours will have passed. Your family probably figures you're still at Sarah's house."

"Is that how it always works out?"

"Um . . . hm." Kay took his hat off so he could scratch his head. "Actually, I'm just going off of what Sarah told me. I mean, if it happened once, it makes sense that it would happen that way again, right? Anyway, Sarah's mom doesn't seem to be all that worried, and both of them need their rest. I mean, I could probably give us wings and fly us there, but just because my spell on Melania worked the way I planned doesn't mean I wouldn't accidentally turn us into bats or ducks or something."

"Okay . . . if we need to wait, we need to wait."

"My thoughts exactly. Besides," his voice got more distant, as though he wasn't speaking to anybody in the room anymore, "I still have a few things to take care of."

"What things?"

Kay looked startled, as though he hadn't meant to say that last part out loud. "Sleep." He stood up suddenly and gave an exaggerated yawn. "I have sleep to take care of. That's the way I say goodnight. Just ask anybody."

"But Kay," Keeley said, "that's not—"

"Anybody but Keeley," Kay added hastily. "Everybody knows you need to talk to dragons differently. It's a sign of respect and all that. Well, good night for now. Take care of sleep and all." Nearly tripping over his robes, Kay scrambled to one of the empty bedrooms and closed the door behind him.

Carrie took Keeley off her shoulder and placed the dragon in the palm of her hand.

"So is that kind of weirdness a boy thing, or . . ."

"No," Keeley said knowingly. "It's a Kay thing."

Carrie took the last empty bedroom. The bed was about as comfortable as the one she had laid on in the palace, but having her freedom made it much more restful. Unfortunately, this time, she didn't want to sleep.

Keeley lay out in the suite, curled up by the embers of the fire like she was a tiny winged dog. Every once in a while, she yelped or said something in her sleep. From the other rooms in the suite, she heard only silence.

She tried to quiet the concerns that kept her awake, but her mind just wouldn't let her be. Instead, she lay on the soft bed, staring up at the ceiling as the night crept slowly by.

Outside, the clock struck midnight. Carrie almost found herself finally drifting off to sleep, but then she heard movement in the suite.

She got out of bed and crept to her door, then put her eye up to the keyhole. In the dull red glow of the embers, she saw Kay tiptoe out of his room. He moved especially quietly around Keeley, making sure not to wake the dragon. Then he slipped out the suite's exit, apparently leaving the companions behind.

Had Carrie been counting the bells outside, she would've noticed that they rang thirteen times, not twelve.

Once Kay had closed the door behind him, Carrie snuck out into the suite. She gently shook Keeley awake. The dragon growled, but Carrie shushed her quickly.

"Keeley," she whispered, holding a finger to her lips. "How's your sense of smell?"

"Very good!" Keeley said cheerfully. Then, catching herself, she started whispering. "Um, Keeley means, very good. She's especially good if there's food at the other end."

"Well, I don't know about food, but something strange is going on." Carrie picked the dragon up and put her on her shoulder. "Let's go."

She paused for a moment, wondering if she should wake up the others before setting out after Kay. Something told her not to, so she decided to let them sleep. After all, this wouldn't take much time. Whatever Kay was up to, how much trouble could he possibly get into?

Knowing that the answer to that question was more than she would have liked, Carrie left the inn with Keeley, determined to follow Kay's trail.

Twenty-Four

Every part of Sarah's body felt like it was being pulled away from the rest. She thought the agony would never end. When it finally stopped, she dropped into unconsciousness. Part of her hoped she wouldn't wake up.

She did come to hours later, but at first, she wasn't sure if she was really alive. She couldn't see or hear anything. She knew she was lying down, and she thought she felt shackles around her wrists and ankles. But she didn't dare move.

Still, she was very happy to find out she was still alive.

"Thank goodness," she said out loud, dismayed to find that she still spoke with Melania's voice. "Kay's spell didn't work."

"My spell worked just fine, you witch."

A bright light nearly blinded her, and Sarah found herself in some sort of dungeon. Her cell was only a few feet across on either side. Iron shackles held her by the arms and legs, and silver bars lined her cage on all sides.

Bathed in a white light that emerged from the tip of his staff, Kay looked like a complete stranger to her. The bumbling apprentice was gone, replaced by somebody who seemed utterly joyless and who was wrestling with one of the most difficult decisions of his life.

"Kay, you have to listen to me! I—"

"Be quiet!" Kay shouted.

Sarah obeyed. She knew she needed to defend herself, but she couldn't seem to bring herself to do so. Seeing somebody who'd been so close to her now look at her with such deep hatred stunned her to silence.

"This is the tower my father, Argal, used when he caught spell-casting criminals. Those chains have been used to hold dangerous fey, and the bars will make any spell you cast rebound back on you. This place hasn't been used for years, so even if I left you here to rot, you'd starve to death long before anybody found you."

Kay had entered through an iron-bound door that seemed to serve as the prison's main exit. He walked down three stone steps and came to a stop about ten paces away from the cell. He kept his staff pointed at Sarah the entire time as though it was a gun and she was a dangerous criminal.

"But I'm not going to leave you here," he said. "I hesitated when I fired the ray at you. I transported you here instead of finishing you off. It got you away from Sarah, but it's better than you deserve."

Sarah felt her palms sweat. "Kay, you're making a terrible mistake. I'm Sarah! Melania played a trick on all of us!"

"Shut! Up!" Kay yelled, his face red and his lips trembling. "Everybody in Greystone Valley fell for your tricks. You can't use your magic to weasel your way out of this now, and nothing you say will change what I'm about to do."

The chains at Sarah's wrists rattled as her arms shook in fear—not over the fact that she was about to die, but at the realization of who was going to finish her. "After all we've been through, we can't let it end like this."

"You brainwashed the people of my homeland. You devastated the Great City. You killed my friend Dax, and you would have killed Sarah if I hadn't stopped you. You deserve to die."

Sarah slumped in her cage as she realized what it felt like to be truly helpless. Hatred stopped reason. Even if she did manage to explain, Kay's anger would keep him from realizing she was telling the truth.

"You deserve to die," Kay repeated. The tip of his staff shook, and tears started to roll down his face. "So why can't I do it? What makes me so weak?"

He let the staff go. As it clattered on the ground, Kay sank to his knees and put his head in his hands. Sarah tried to reach out to comfort him, but the chains kept her well away from her troubled friend.

"Maybe it's not weakness that keeps you from being a killer," a gentle voice said. "Maybe it's really a strength."

Carrie stepped through the iron door and walked down the stairs. Keeley flew by her side and started circling the room, keeping her fierce emerald eyes locked on Sarah.

"How did you find me?" Kay whispered.

"Keeley helped!" the energetic dragon cried. She landed on the ground and nuzzled against Kay's purple clothes. "She knows the smell of sweaty robes and ash caused by miscast magic very well, and she was able to track you all the way through the Great City!" The dragon turned to face the cell and arched her back. "And she sees that you need help. Melania must be dealt with, and Keeley will do it for you!"

"Will you really, Keeley?" the boy asked. "*Can* you?"

The chains rattled again as Sarah grabbed the bars and shook them with all her might. "Please—one of you has to listen to me!"

The dragon growled and breathed in, seemingly ready to spit fire right through the bars of Sarah's cage. But then she sighed and nothing more than smoke came out.

"No," she admitted. "Keeley can't. In battle, it would be different. But not like this."

Despite her situation, Sarah couldn't help but feel proud of her friends for their mercy. Put in their place, she feared that she would have made the opposite decision, which would have resulted in the death of somebody she cared about.

Carrie stood up and looked angrily at Sarah. "I hope you like being in a cell like this," she said. "Your accommodations aren't as nice as mine were, but putting a bowl of fruit in the room doesn't excuse you from making somebody a prisoner."

"Carrie," she said, "I'm not the person who captured you. I was winning the fight against Melania. Then she went and pulled some sort of switcheroo to make me look like her and her look like me."

Carrie shook her head. "That doesn't make any sense. Sarah's mom would have seen right through a trick like that."

"Are you sure? My mom's smart, but she's not perfect."

For a very long time, nobody in the dungeon so much as breathed. Each of Sarah's friends were weighing the possible truth behind her story, and Sarah was coming to the realization that this whole encounter would probably end with her chained and abandoned in a dungeon for the rest of her life.

Finally, Carrie asked the others, "What if she's telling the truth?"

Kay shook his head. "It can't be. Why would Melania go from being somebody who had a whole city under her control to somebody who has to deal with math tests every Friday?"

"Maybe we should ask her something only Sarah would know," Carrie said.

"Or maybe I could cast some sort of truth spell on her," Kay replied. "I mean, I don't know of one off the top of my head, but I'm sure I could guess . . ."

"No, you idiot!" Sarah yelled. "You'd wind up erasing your memory again or changing things so you can never tell a lie or some stupid thing like that!"

Kay scratched the back of his neck. "See? That's something I could imagine Sarah saying. Then again, that's also something I could imagine anybody who's seen me cast multiple spells saying."

"There's got to be a logical way to figure this out," Carrie said. "Let's think. Hm . . . for starters, everybody up above is out of Melania's control."

"So?" Kay asked.

"You said this cage bounces spells back at the person who casts them. Would that cancel out the spells she already cast? I mean, we assumed everybody was free because Melania was dead. But whether this person here is telling the truth or not, we know she's still alive."

"I don't think it would break the spells she's already cast," Kay admitted. "But I'm not really an expert on how this works. My father kind of got run out of the city by suspicious townsfolk before he explained . . . well, really anything at all about magic."

While Carrie and Kay tried to puzzle their way through the mystery, Keeley squeezed through the bars and sniffed. Running on all fours, she scurried up Sarah's dress and came to rest on her shoulder. Despite the situation, Sarah felt her body relax slightly as she felt Keeley's tiny claws—during the course of their adventures, the dragon climbing up to perch on her shoulder had become a welcome sensation. Whether she noticed this or not, Keeley sunk her claws into the clothing experimentally before curling up comfortably next to Sarah's ear.

"Keeley believes her!" the dragon cried. "No matter what shape she wears, she has the most comfortable shoulder!"

"Okay," Carrie said with some amusement. "That's one vote for trusting her."

Thinking about the situation, Sarah decided that she needed to give some input of her own. "It doesn't matter whether you believe me or not. Just leave me here and find the person you think is Sarah. If you guys are all down here, that means Melania's disguised as me and alone with my mom right now. Who knows what she might do?"

"Sarah or not, she's right," Carrie said. "If she really is Melania, then there's no harm in telling Sarah about the situation. And if she's not, that means we need to stop the real Melania before she does something terrible."

Kay spent some time thinking. Then the conflict drained out of his face, replaced by the same bumbling cockiness that Sarah had always seen there. He picked up his staff and pointed it at the cage. With a word, the shackles came undone and the door swung open.

"If Keeley trusts you, that's good enough for me," he said.

"Thank you," Sarah said.

She stepped out of the cage and was surprised when Kay threw himself forward, hugging her tightly and burying his face into her shoulder.

"I'm sorry," he said. "I'm sorry for what I almost did to you."

The hug felt strange to Sarah, partly because she was in an adult form and was thus taller than Kay for a change. Nonetheless, she felt that it was very important for her to return the hug. She embraced her friend as tightly as she could, almost fearing she was going to hurt him.

"It's okay," she said. "I knew you'd never hurt me."

Kay pulled away from the embrace and smiled. "You lie like Sarah does," he said. "Badly."

Getting out of the prison was easy, but sneaking across town was more difficult—Sarah happened to look like the woman who had turned the entire city into slaves. Luckily, by hunching her shoulders and keeping her head down, she was able to go from being regal in appearance to somebody who just blended in with the background. Nonetheless, the companions rushed back to the inn as quickly as they could for fear that somebody was going to recognize her.

The embers were still glowing in the fireplace when they returned to the suite. The doors to each bedroom were closed, and there was no immediate sign that anybody had come or gone since Carrie and Keeley left to follow Kay.

Kay threw open the door to the room where the last two companions should have been sleeping peacefully. It was empty. Only a single wand remained behind.

Twenty-Five

inda woke up in another world. No . . . she woke up in her world. Why did she think she'd been somewhere else?

She lay in her large, soft bed wearing a light-gray nightgown. She'd kicked the blankets off sometime during the night because the whole house felt unusually warm for the fall. Draped across the foot of her bed was her fluffy green bathrobe. She sat up, swung her legs out of the bed, and picked up the robe.

Something looked different. Hadn't she worn something like this not too long ago?

No, of course not.

"Sarah?" she called to a house that seemed larger and emptier than it had been before. "Are you up?"

No answer. Maybe her daughter was sulking in her bedroom. After all, she'd just been grounded for . . .

For what?

Linda held a hand to her head. Maybe she was getting sick. "Better get your head in the game, lady," she muttered to herself.

She put on a pair of slippers and left her bedroom. Sarah's room was down the hall on the right. She'd left her door open. Linda poked her head in. There was nobody inside.

That seemed odd. Sarah always kept it shut tight as though she were guarding some secret lost treasure in there among her books and magazines.

Linda smiled. As though the girl could keep secrets from her mother.

By the time she got to the stairs, she was met by a delicious and unmistakable smell. Bacon, eggs, and . . . was that coffee? Where would Sarah have learned how to brew coffee?

Linda checked the calendar in her mind. It was September—her birthday wasn't for another seven months, and Mother's Day was even later than that. So why was Sarah suddenly trying to butter her up?

"What's the special occasion?" she asked when she reached the kitchen. Sure enough, Sarah was in there, wearing her blue pajamas and working some sort of kitchen magic that Linda had never thought her to be capable of. In addition to frying bacon, cooking an omelet, and brewing some fresh coffee, she was in the midst of mixing a sauce that looked like it combined maple syrup, brown sugar, vinegar, and marmalade.

Sarah grinned from ear to ear. "What special occasion? This is just breakfast."

The look Linda gave her daughter combined equal parts gratitude and suspicion. "Don't give me that. I've never seen you use the stove in your life." The bacon started to pop, and Linda instinctively moved toward it. "Look out, it's going to—"

Sarah moved expertly, cutting Linda off and flipping the bacon before it started to burn. Then she poured the sauce she'd been preparing on top. The pan sizzled loudly and let off a lot of steam, but the delicious aroma that came from it was almost irresistible.

"I've got this, Mom," Sarah said cheerfully. "You sit down and relax. I'll have breakfast ready in a minute."

Linda shrugged her shoulders and gave up. Whatever her daughter had planned, she would just have to wait and see.

They usually ate together on the small kitchen table, but Sarah had covered that with bowls, plates, and utensils. The dining room, which was normally only used if they had company over, now had place settings for three people.

Ah . . . that explained it. Carrie was probably coming over for breakfast. *Or,* Linda thought with a mixture of optimism and worry, *maybe she has a boyfriend.*

She sat at the table, folded her hands together, and furrowed her brow in thought. She'd experienced this feeling a lot lately—the feeling that there was something on the edge of her mind that needed to be remembered but that she couldn't quite grasp. The harder she tried to chase the memory, the faster it seemed to run.

The actual memory continually escaped her, but the emotion didn't. The harder she thought, the sadder she became. It was like she had lost something—no, had lost some*one*. By the time Sarah came out of the kitchen with a cup of coffee for her, Linda was almost in tears.

"What's wrong?" Sarah's question was almost hysterically panicked, as though she'd just walked in to find a giant spider instead of a sad-looking mom.

"Nothing, sweetie," Linda said, rubbing a hand across her eyes. "I was just daydreaming."

Sarah put the coffee down on the table and then dove toward her mom, giving a long, tight hug.

"It's okay, darling," Linda said. "Really. I'm just not myself this morning."

Sarah let go and smiled. "You'll be better soon."

"As soon as I've had a sip of my coffee."

Linda took a drink and gasped in surprise. She'd expected the coffee to taste bitter and maybe even a little burned—a nice gesture from her daughter, but one that was doomed to failure thanks to her inexperience. But this drink was perfect. It had just the right amount of cream in it and a slight taste of cinnamon and hazelnut.

"Who are you and what have you done with my daughter?" Linda asked. "I've hardly ever seen you cook in your life, let alone make something like this." She sniffed the air. The rest of the breakfast smelled like it was going to be even better.

"I'm saying thank you," Sarah said.

"Thank you for what?"

"For everything." Sarah waved her arms around the house, then toward her mom as though she were performing a simple dance. "I have everything I ever wanted. And it's not enough for me to just live that life the way I used to. I want to be the perfect daughter for you."

"Sweetie, you've always been—"

"No, she . . . no, I haven't," Sarah interrupted. "I've fought with you, I've lied to you, and I've disobeyed you. But I'm going to fix things. I'm going to give us both everything we've ever wanted."

Linda looked at her daughter with growing concern. Something seemed to be bothering Sarah, and a strange feeling of dread started to creep into her own heart.

"Sarah, you've obviously overworked yourself this morning. Sit down and let me finish making breakfast. You look like you could use a little rest."

"No, Mom. I'm fine. I just got a bit carried away. You relax. Let me do this for you."

"Really, honey. Your friend will be coming over any moment now and—"

"My friend?"

"You placed three spots at the table."

"That's your other surprise, Mom."

Linda took another sip of her coffee and then pushed herself away from the table. "You're still not making much sense," she said in a more authoritative voice. "You've obviously put a lot of thought into this, and I appreciate it. But you also need to calm down for a bit. Let me take it from here."

"No, Mom. Sit down!" The outburst came so sharply and so suddenly that Linda found herself following her daughter's directions more out of shock than anything else. Sarah looked shocked too, like she'd slapped herself across the face. "It's okay. I'm okay. Please, just wait for your surprise. It'll be perfect. I promise."

Linda heard footsteps crunching across the dead leaves outside. Somebody walked up the steps of the front porch and opened the door without knocking.

She looked questioningly at Sarah. Her daughter glowed with anticipation, as though everything she'd ever wanted for Christmas was about to walk right through the door.

"I'm home!" a man's voice said.

Linda's heart almost stopped.

A bearded man with brown hair that had just started to turn gray walked into the dining room. He'd taken his shoes off when he came into the house, which was something Linda had told him to do again and again but which he had never actually done while he was alive. Sarah clapped her hands excitedly. Linda stood up and walked forward wordlessly, like she was in a dream.

Yes, this had to be a dream. Because there in front of her was her husband. But he was gone. He had been . . .

Had been what? Where had he gone? Linda's head felt foggy. The back of her skull seemed to burn, as though Sarah's eyes were boring into her mind. Memories escaped from her like sand through a sieve. As they did, she felt happier, more content, but also empty.

No, her husband wasn't dead. That had all been a bad dream. This was reality.

She smiled and walked forward happily to give her husband a kiss on the lips. But she slowed again as she got closer. This wasn't right.

The man in front of her looked phony, with a smile painted on his face and the tips of his teeth showing. He just stood there, not moving toward her, not saying anything, waiting for Linda to come to him. And now that she looked at him more closely, he didn't even look like a real person. He looked fuzzy around the edges, like . . .

Like a photograph.

Linda's eyes fell across the family portrait that sat on the dining room table—the one they had taken three years ago for their Christmas card. The picture had come out a little blurry. Everybody was fuzzy around the edges. Just like her husband was now.

It hadn't been a bad dream. This was the dream. And while it had started nicely, it was quickly turning into a nightmare.

She turned away from the man who wasn't her husband and looked at Sarah.

"What are you doing?" she whispered.

As soon as she said those words, she knew the truth. This person in front of her wasn't her daughter. But she wasn't an illusion like the man who had just entered the room. Somebody had taken her daughter's place.

"*Uermo lia lectus.*" Sarah's wand came out as soon as she saw the suspicion creep across her mom's face.

Linda stumbled forward and dropped to her knees. She tried to say something, but the words never left her tongue. She fell face-down on the carpet and drifted off into slumber.

Melania waved her hand, and Linda's husband disappeared into smoke.

"It wasn't perfect after all," she said sadly. She knelt down by Linda's sleeping form and touched her hair. She looked like a slumbering angel. That made her an angel's daughter.

"Don't worry, Mom," she said. "I'll try again. I'll get it right. Sooner or later, we're going to live the perfect life together. You'll see."

Twenty-Six

Something had to break, either Sarah's hand or the table she was hitting. She didn't care; she didn't own either.

"*Ebuo lurecu hiaas!*" She shouted the words to the transformation spell for the fourth time.

Nothing happened. She pounded the table again.

"You're definitely Sarah," Kay commented.

"What's that supposed to mean?" From Melania's body, Sarah shot a venomous glare.

"Nothing much. It's just that I don't know of too many people who think with their fists so often."

"I can't seem to think at all!" She threw up her arms and stomped about the room where her mom should've been. "A transformation spell is the first one I ever cast. I should know it like the back of my hand. So why can't I cast it to get back to my original form?"

Keeley, who'd perched on Sarah's shoulder, sniffed at her. "Keeley hates to point out the obvious," she stated, "but the back of your hand is very unfamiliar."

"She's right," Kay said. "You're obviously not yourself—in more ways than one."

"Well that's just great!" Sarah threw up her arms. "How am I supposed to convince my mom that I'm the good one when I look like the person who erased her memory?"

"Perception isn't everything," Carrie said.

Sarah looked at her friend as though she were speaking a completely different language. "What did you say?"

"Perception isn't everything," Carrie repeated.

"But that's all Melania talked about. She kept going on about how her illusions were stronger than my spells because they changed people's perceptions. And you know what? She was right."

"Except she wasn't," Kay said.

"Of course she was!" Sarah yelled. "She's there, and we're here with no idea of how to save my mom."

"No," Kay said firmly. "She was wrong. If perception was everything, we wouldn't have let you out of that cell. We had no reason to trust you other than Keeley's intuition. So we know illusions only go so far. Now we have to figure out how far Melania and your mom might have gone."

"Well, that's sort of the problem," Carrie said. "They could be anywhere by now."

Kay stroked his chin thoughtfully. "Well, the good news is, Greystone Valley isn't that big of a land. If they're somewhere here, we should be able to find them easily. We've got contacts among the dwarves, fey, and dragons of the valley. Sure, some of them might not be happy to see us—well, most of them won't, actually—but if the choice is between us and Melania, I like our chances of convincing them to side with us, even if it's only for a little while. On the other hand . . ."

"Oh boy . . . what's the bad news?" Carrie asked.

"It's a small valley, but it's a big universe. If Melania somehow gets Sarah's mom all the way to Castle Greystone, well . . ."

" . . . she could be anywhere," a despondent Sarah said. "It'll be like trying to find a needle in a haystack."

"That's not quite true," Kay said. "It's more like trying to find a single needle in an infinite number of haystacks . . . which, now that I say it out loud, is quite a bit worse."

"We have to assume they're going to Castle Greystone," Sarah said, "and if they're far ahead of us, we have to find a way to find out which door they're going through."

"Maybe we should just sit at the castle's entrance and wait for your mom to fight her own way out," Carrie said hopefully. "We've already seen what she can do."

Sarah thought about what her mom had shown in battle. With patience and skill, she'd almost brought an entire city to its knees. If it came down to strength versus strength, her mom would certainly win.

But . . .

"It's not strength against strength," Sarah said. "The whole situation plays into Melania's hands. My mom doesn't know who the enemy really is."

Out of ideas and out of patience, Sarah stormed past her friends and left the room. The others rushed after her as she stomped down the stairs and out of the inn.

"Sarah," Keeley said urgently, "don't you remember who you look like?"

Carrie grabbed the wand that Sarah's mom had left behind and rushed after Kay and Keeley, who were scrambling to keep up with Sarah.

"Yeah," Kay said, his eyes darting back and forth as he made sure that nobody was in the city streets at this early hour of the morning. "If the locals see you the way you are right now, they're going to think—"

"Sabrina!" Sarah yelled at the top of her lungs. Some of the darkened windows came to life as people lit candles in search of the source of the shouting. "Sabrina, I know you can hear me! If you don't answer me, you'll never see your granddaughter again!"

"*Adias delet*!" Kay shouted, waving his staff wildly.

The candles in the windows all went out, but so did the moon and stars. At Kay's command, every light source in the entire city—maybe even the entire valley—winked out.

Sarah whirled around to where she thought Kay might be, hissing venomously through the blackness all around her, "What did you do that for?"

Kay's voice came defensively through the darkness. "Don't get mad at me! You're the one who nearly got yourself attacked by an angry mob!"

"He's right," Carrie said. "People were just celebrating Melania's death. If they see her stomping through the streets and yelling like a crazy woman, they're going to try to finish the job."

"I don't care what they do," Sarah snarled. "I need to find my mom, and the only person who might be able to help is—"

"Sarah," Keeley whispered. "Look!"

Two tiny points of green light appeared in the otherwise endless blackness surrounding the friends. Sarah felt Keeley on her shoulder, and she felt the dragon's body tense the way it always did when fey creatures came near.

Having gotten the attention they wanted, the faeries darted away, leaving a trail like a pair of green ribbons made of light behind them. Without thinking twice, Sarah dashed after them. After a few seconds, she moved outside the cloud of darkness Kay had conjured up, noting with some relief that it didn't extend through the entire city the way as she originally thought. She didn't care about the shouts of alarm or the panicked cries as people recognized Melania's form. In fact, she was so focused on following the two fey that she didn't even notice her own friends chasing after her.

The fey darted nimbly through the streets, giggling at the merry chase. Only when their lights winked out and they seemed to vanish did Sarah realize where they had led her—right to the base of the clock tower. And the door was open.

Up until now, Sarah had only seen the tower in the distance, looming on the horizon like some giant stone guardian. Examining it up close, she realized the face glowed so it could be seen even at night. As massive as the tower was, it didn't seem to have any entrances or exits except the eight-foot-tall arched door at its base. Despite the fact that the fey had obviously led her to the building on purpose, Sarah felt hesitant to step in without preparing herself first. For a change, it was her friends who pushed her on without looking.

"Go, go, go!" Carrie yelled, shoving her in the back. "Move, move, move!"

Keeley grabbed Sarah's arm and pulled. That combined with Carrie's pushing got her through the door. Behind her, shouts of alarm and the clang of weapons and armor came up the streets.

"Stay back!" Kay shouted to the assembled mob. "We've dealt with Melania before, and we'll do it again!"

Recognizing one of their newest heroes, the citizens of the Great City stopped before storming the clock tower and trying to kill Sarah themselves. Stepping into the tower, Kay slammed the door behind him, leaving the companions alone with whatever might be waiting for them inside.

Twenty-Seven

"**O**h my lovely Linda . . . look what you've done to your fair face."

Sarah squinted her eyes as she tried to make out Sabrina's shape in the darkness. "I'm not Linda!" she yelled. "I'm . . . wait a minute. Why didn't you call me Melania?"

A clicking, grinding noise echoed throughout the tower. The lights of Sabrina's fey followers appeared as a pair of green dots high up near the ceiling. Then the swirling star-like patterns of Sabrina's eyes came into view, illuminating the rest of the building. The clock tower was filled with complex gears that seemed to be made of gold, silver, and other precious metals. A few rusty-looking metal ladders led to platforms higher up in the tower, but for the most part, the entire place seemed to be dedicated to just holding the massive inner workings of the great clock. Sarah was hardly an expert on the subject, but there seemed to be more gears and wheels here than what was needed to run even a timepiece as big as this one.

Levers bent and bells chimed as the clockwork twisted around to serve as Sabrina's newest form. In a few seconds, the companions stood staring up at a pair of glowing flywheels that served as eyes and a floating row of cogs that formed a makeshift mouth. Sabrina's temporary head looked to be about twenty feet wide. Since she'd formed about halfway up the great tower, the friends at the bottom had to crane their necks to look at her.

"You only look like Melania, dear one. But appearance actually accounts for little. I know my granddaughter when I look at her."

"Well, at least she knows what family you belong to," Kay whispered.

Sabrina's clockwork eyes turned toward the purple-clad boy as soon as he spoke up. "And you've brought a fascinating friend with you, haven't you? Adorable Argal . . . have you kept that sensational spellbook safe?"

Kay's face flushed at the mention of his father's name, not to mention the spellbook which had been destroyed more than a year ago. "Um . . . well, I, er . . ."

"Relax, my dear," Sabrina said. "Even very old things can get damaged or misplaced."

"Misplaced is right," Sarah interrupted, "but it's not a thing that's gone missing. It's my mom."

The creaking and groaning from above fell silent as the gears which formed Sabrina's mouth stopped moving. The eyes flickered and readjusted as though the ghost was taking in her surroundings anew. Then, with a rusty-sounding clatter, she began to speak again.

"Oh my . . . how horrifically harrowing. It seems that the manipulative Melania has more treacherous tricks up her sleeve than I previously believed."

"That's right. She took my mom, and we don't know where!"

The eyes rolled upward as Sabrina glanced into the long darkness that led to the top of the clock tower. Then, her voice more thoughtful, she said, "Did any of you happen to count the chimes at midnight?"

Sarah raised her eyebrows quizzically. Kay and Carrie shrugged while Keeley simply shook her head.

"A pity. So many people lack the lost lore of this tower. It grants wishes, you see, but only if the timing is right."

"But what does that have to do with my mom?" Sarah shouted.

"What time did my lovely, lost Linda disappear?"

"I don't know . . . I was in a cell then."

Kay scratched the back of his neck. "I was sort of planning to . . . kill you . . . so I didn't pay much attention to the time, either."

Carrie closed her eyes in thought for a moment, trying to recall every detail she possibly could. Finally, she opened her eyes and said, "Midnight. It was exactly midnight when Keeley and I left to follow Kay, and we haven't seen Sarah's mom since."

The giant glowing orbs turned their attention toward Carrie. "And how many times did the bells chime?"

"Um . . . I don't know. Twelve, I guess."

"No, my dear. They chimed thirteen times. And that means that somebody's wish was granted."

"So what was Melania wishing for?" Sarah asked.

"I think she wants to be you," Carrie said. "When I was her prisoner, she kept talking about wanting a friend—everybody in her own world treated her like a threat. She's been focused on you ever since you came here, and she must be amazed at what she sees. I mean, think about it. You're magical just like her, but instead of people fearing you, you've got all these friends. Me and Keeley and Kay and . . . and your mom."

"So, if she wants to be me, then she must have gone back to my home with my mom. That was her wish, wasn't it?"

The gears above shifted into a crooked smile. "Who can say for sure, my dear? Like all wily women, the mind of Melania is a mystery." The voice became more serious, losing some of the patronizing, grandmotherly tone that Sabrina always seemed to have. "But if you think you know where she went, you need to follow her. I allow my lovely Emerald Enchantresses to leave this valley with the knowledge that they will come back. But to be as awful as to abscond with them without my beneficent blessing . . . she must face my granddaughter's righteous wrath if she did that."

Sarah touched Kay on the shoulder. "Do you have a spell that can bring us back to Castle Greystone?"

"I used to have a transport spell that could take us anywhere in the valley," Kay responded, "but it was in my father's spellbook. I haven't tried to cast it since, so it might not—"

"Don't worry, my lovelies," Sabrina interrupted. "Just make a wish."

The eyes disappeared, and the fey vanished with them. With a groan and a clank, the gears returned to their rightful place and started turning again, allowing the great magical clock to keep time. But no sooner had they started moving than they ground to a halt. Then they turned backward at a frightening speed.

"What's happening now?" Carrie yelled over the din.

The clock struck one, but it was well past one o'clock by then. Sarah stroked Keeley under the chin, then grabbed both Carrie and Kay by the hands.

"It seems our fond farewell comes far earlier than I had hoped," Sabrina's disembodied voice said. "But if you can rescue lovely Linda, I have fervent faith that you will both return to me someday soon. Now, my wily wanderers . . . make a wish."

She could hear the giant hands at the top of the tower whirling backwards. After a few minutes, the gears started to slow. Then they started to move forward again, right at the stroke of midnight.

One, two, three. The clanging of the chimes echoed so loudly through the tower that Sarah felt her teeth rattle.

Four, five, six. She pictured herself with her wand raised, ready for the final battle.

Seven, eight, nine. She closed her eyes and saw her mom's gentle face.

Ten, eleven, twelve. Suddenly, an unwanted moment of doubt jumped into her mind. She wasn't herself, literally or figuratively. What if she didn't have what it took to beat Melania?

She pushed the doubts to the back of her mind and made her wish—a wish not only to be by her mom's side, but to also have the strength to finish Melania off once and for all.

Then the bell rang a thirteenth time. Sarah and her friends felt themselves whisked away as though a giant invisible hand had flung them out of the tower, into the sky, and clear over the horizon.

They came down more gently than seemed possible. Since each of the companions had closed their eyes, they didn't know if they'd been spirited away magically or just tossed through time and space by some giant, ghostly hand. Nonetheless, the four friends found themselves in front of the hulking, rocky form of Castle Greystone.

"Wait a minute!" Sarah yelled. "This isn't what I wished! I wanted to be with my mom, not at the front door!"

"It's okay," Kay said. "We're most of the way there, at least."

"Yeah . . . unless Melania's got another trick in store! I thought the thirteenth chime was supposed to grant a wish!"

"Well, maybe there are limits to the wish's power. Castle Greystone has a lot of magical defenses of its own."

"It's Keeley's fault," the tiny dragon said.

Sarah looked at the dragon, who brushed up against Sarah's ankles.

"Keeley wants to help like the rest of you, but she didn't wish to go further than here. If wicked Melania is inside the castle, Keeley can't follow."

"She's not really inside," Kay said. "She's through one of the doors."

"It doesn't matter," the dragon insisted. "Don't you remember, Kay? Dragons made a pact with the wizard of the castle and swore we would never enter. Keeley wants to see this through, but the pact of the dragons was made by Queen Adlin herself—it's much older than young Keeley, yes it is."

"What if you weren't a dragon?" Carrie interjected.

Keeley looked shocked at the very suggestion and wrapped her tail around herself defensively. "Why, then, Keeley wouldn't look as pretty as she does today!"

"That's not what I meant. Has any dragon ever tried to have a wizard change their shape before they entered? What if you were a cat or a mouse or a bird? Then, technically, you wouldn't be breaking any rules, and we could change you back as soon as we were out of the castle."

Kay, Keeley, and Sarah each got a perplexed look on their face.

"It can't be that simple," Kay said. "Can it?"

"There's only one way to find out," Carrie said. "What do you think, Keeley?"

Smoke trailed from Keeley's nostrils as she considered Carrie's solution. "Keeley wants to try it. But Sarah, make sure you make her something dangerous like she is now!" The dragon bared her teeth, giving a demonstration of the many small but painful needle-like fangs that awaited her foes.

Sarah pointed her finger at Keeley, preparing the spell in her mind. But just before she started casting, she dropped her hand to her side and shook her head.

"You do it, Kay."

Kay titled his hat backward so he could scratch his head. "Are you sure? I mean, the last time I cast a transformation spell . . ."

"You have to be the one to do it," Sarah insisted.

"Why?" Carrie asked. "Magic is the thing you do best!"

"It's been a very long time since I cast a transformation spell that worked," Sarah said. "And I don't have a spellbook anymore to double check it. I don't have a wand to help focus my magic. And . . ." She waved her hands wildly, emphasizing that they weren't really her hands. "I'm not me anymore! I don't want to mess things up any more than I already have."

Kay put his staff on the ground and folded his arms. "I'm not going to cast the spell," he said. "You need to do it."

"Come on!" Sarah yelled. "Now's not the time—"

"Now's the perfect time! If you can't do this, why are we running off into another world to face Melania? You've got magic in your blood and in your mind. It's the thing you were born to do. A book and a wand are helpful, but they're really just old pages and a crooked stick."

"But I can't afford to mess up right now," Sarah insisted. "What if I cast a spell and turn Keeley into stone or something?"

"Come on—that's something I do, not you! I've never really been able to control my spells, but I keep on trying anyway. And you know what? I'm getting a lot better because I'm willing to take those risks. Sure, there are the times when I've turned myself into a frog or turned inanimate objects into snakes or added a few extra eyes or toes to somebody. . ."

"Or thrown us a city block away while lighting a building on fire," Carrie added.

"Or flooded a tunnel," Keeley joined in. "Or made your nose grow or—"

"That's enough," Kay interrupted. "The point is, I keep trying, and I've helped us out because of that. If you don't have the confidence for this one spell, how can you expect to save your mom when you need to?"

Sarah considered the situation. A sharp, cold breeze whipped through the area, making her shiver. Then she realized that she'd been shaking before the breeze picked up.

"Okay," she said, trying to quell her fear. "Here goes nothing."

Kay picked up his staff and took a couple of steps away from Keeley. Then he stepped forward again, touched Carrie on the arm, and encouraged her to do the same.

"Just in case," he whispered. "Trust me—I know the proper distance you need to be at to avoid a spell backfire."

Sarah took a deep breath and pointed her finger at Keeley again. "*Ebuo lurecu hiaas!*"

Keeley's body began to change shape as though she were made of putty. In a panic, she shut her eyes, afraid to look at what sort of mixed-up monster she'd turned her friend into.

Instead of the sounds of disaster, Sarah heard Carrie give an affectionate squeal.

"Why, Keeley, what big ears you have!"

Sarah opened one eye. In Keeley's place was a small, white bunny rabbit.

Keeley whipped her head around and examined her cotton tail.

"Ooo!" In her new form, Keeley sounded even higher-pitched than normal. "This might not be as dangerous as Keeley would have liked, but now she has soft, soft fur!"

"Huh," Kay said. "Usually, a transformation spell doesn't allow somebody who has become an animal to talk. How come when I mess up a spell, it nearly causes a catastrophe, but when you mess up, it makes things work even better?"

Sarah laughed in relief. "Some people have all the luck, I guess."

"Of course Keeley can still talk! She wouldn't be Keeley if she couldn't make her voice heard. And after all . . . a-choo!"

Keeley turned her head away from her companions just in time. A burst of fire shot out of her nostrils as she sneezed, singeing her whiskers and leaving a black scorch mark on the side of Castle Greystone.

"Bunnies aren't supposed to shoot fire," Carrie said.

"Actually, the battle-bunnies of the Firkrag Forest have been known to shoot the occasional fireball," Kay said. "They eat red-hot coals after forest fires to give themselves the fuel. True story."

Sarah crossed her arms. "True story? Really?"

Kay kept a straight face for about half a second. "No," he admitted. "But I thought it was creative of me. Not all my surprises have to be magical, you know."

Sarah picked up the new Keeley-bunny and put her on the familiar perch of her shoulder. "Are we ready to give this a try?" she asked.

Each of the companions nodded and stood by Sarah's side.

With half their number transformed, one inexperienced in battle, and one who only sometimes controlled his spells, Sarah didn't exactly feel confident. But since the alternative was never seeing her mom again, she figured she had no choice but to try.

She took a deep breath. Then she and her three friends stepped into Castle Greystone.

Twenty-Eight

Sarah had walked the long, dark corridor twice before. The most recent time had been the beginning of an adventure. This time felt like an ending . . . either Melania's or hers.

Kay passed a hand over his staff and created a light, just as he'd done before. He didn't get the spell entirely right, as the color of the glow constantly shifted, and his staff now gave off an acrid smoke as though it were burning.

Keeley entered the castle next. The dragon-bunny shivered slightly when she took her first steps through the doorway but relaxed once she got a few steps further in.

Carrie brought up the rear, her mouth wide in amazement as she surveyed the inside of the castle. "Where do all these doors lead?"

"Everywhere," Kay responded. "We can go to any world that Greystone Valley touches, which is all of them, I think."

"Then how do we know which will lead us to Sarah's mom?"

"Sarah can see through the doors without opening them—it's something I don't think anybody else can do. But we don't even need that, because I know exactly which door leads to your world. After all, I've been there."

"Shh!" Sarah said, silencing her companions. Then, in a whisper, she spoke again. "I don't think anybody else is here."

"That's not surprising," Kay said. "The castle's open now, but it's not like it sees a lot of traffic."

"But there should be somebody or something here—a guardian, a trap . . . something! Melania had to have known you three would follow her if she kidnapped my mom."

"Maybe we got lucky," Kay said. "Melania might have underestimated us. She didn't know you were still alive, so maybe she figured the rest of us wouldn't be able to get back here."

Sarah nodded in response, but she didn't feel too hopeful that Kay was right. Melania had planned everything so thoroughly . . .

Actually, no. She hadn't planned it. She couldn't have known that Kay would accidentally cancel her memory charm or that Dax would defeat Grimjaw. Melania didn't plan—she adapted, and she always seemed to turn the worst situations to her advantage. And if she knew Kay had found his way into Sarah's world before, why would she leave a loose end now?

Sarah touched the door, and images of her world flooded into her mind. She pushed past them, searching for one image in particular— her home. Melania had taken her life, so she must have taken her home as well. But just as she feared, the house was empty. Neither Melania nor her mom were on the other side.

"It's a dead end," she moaned.

The companions stared at each other, their faces pale. They looked at the countless doors around them. Castle Greystone had never seemed bigger or more intimidating.

"All right," Kay said after a long period of time. "We'll each pick a door. Look in, then shut the door if what's on the other side is too dangerous to handle on your own. We'll look everywhere."

Sarah glanced down the seemingly endless row of doors, then looked up at the balcony above her where even more worlds waited.

"Everywhere?" she asked skeptically.

"Whatever it takes to find your mom," Kay said firmly.

"It's not that easy," Sarah said. "I can see through the doors, but I don't see the whole world at once. Not only would we have to find the right door, but we'd need to look through the whole planet to find my mom. Unless we know what to look for, we'll die of old age long before we find her."

"Shadows," Carrie said cryptically.

"What?" Sarah asked.

Carrie grinned. "It's crazy. I never thought being held captive would turn out to be useful. When Melania was talking to me, she kept telling me how she came from a world where magic was rare, like you and I do. But she didn't hide her magic like you do at school. She used it openly, and people turned against her. They called her a witch and hunted her. And they exiled her to a world of shadows."

"What's that got to do with . . . hmm." Sarah bit her own question back and turned Carrie's words over in her mind. People really hunted Melania for casting a few spells? Surely that wouldn't have happened to her . . . or was that why her mom always told her not to use her magic in public?

"There's more than that," Carrie said, excitement rising in her voice. "She learned how to control those shadows, how to shape them. The people in her old world thought they threw her into a prison, but they just made her more powerful. So if you were her, looking for a way to disappear to a place where you don't want anybody to follow you—"

"You'd go back to where you were strongest," Sarah said. She brightened up. "So now we know what to look for."

"It's still going to take a while," Kay said, eyeing the rows of doors before them.

"It's better than needing to explore whole planets," Sarah responded.

"Then we will be heroes!" Keeley cried, stomping her broad feet. "Wicked Melania will pay for her misdeeds, larger version of Sarah will be saved, and Dax will not have died in vain! Let's go!"

The dragon-bunny hopped so quickly down the hallway that she almost got lost in the darkness beyond Kay's light.

Sarah found herself lost between worlds for what seemed like hours. Every door she touched showed her different images. Some showed her shining spires and fantastic creatures, and she made a mental note to travel there someday. Others showed her nightmarish visions and utter despair, and she could only hope that those memories would fade away as time went on.

The companions stood behind her every step of the way, ready to jump through a door at a moment's notice. But with each new door she touched, Sarah became more and more convinced that her mom was lost forever.

Then she touched a door and saw nothing but darkness.

"This might be it," she whispered, her mouth dry.

She pressed her hand firmly against the wood and concentrated. She focused more deeply on the images that came to her. Her mind pushed through the shadows until shapes started to appear. Her palms sweating, she concentrated even more, and the shadows began to lift.

Suddenly, she saw daylight. More than that, she saw her home.

Her house looked better than it ever had, but everything around it seemed like an empty canvas. There were trees and hills as well as the city where she went to school looming on the horizon, but none of them seemed real. If this world had been a picture, her home would've been painted with care and love, but the artist had only used a few brushstrokes for everything else. Maybe a home was all Melania wanted. Or maybe she was still getting the hang of recreating the rest of Sarah's life so she could steal it all away.

Sarah didn't need to look back at her friends to know they were ready. Without hesitation, she flung open the door and stepped into Melania's world.

Everything seemed foggy at first. She felt dizzy as the cosmos whirled around her, magically whisking her away to another world. She almost fell over but somehow kept her balance. Then the world grew solid around her again, and she and her companions found themselves in her living room—or rather, a place that looked identical to it.

Everything in her home seemed to be recreated perfectly, right down to the stain on the carpet where she spilled grape juice when she was younger. The sun was setting outside, and Sarah's mom sat in her rocking chair, thumbing through a magazine. The companions entered silently enough that she didn't notice them for a second. Then she let out a gasp, dropped her magazine, and stood up in alarm.

"You!" Sarah's mom seemed to react more on instinct than memory, for her eyes had that familiar look of forgetfulness that had plagued them both over the past few months. But the memories didn't take long to come back, and her eyes cleared. "Melania," she said, reminding herself of the name of her foe. "What have you done to Sarah's friends?"

"Mom!" A voice that Sarah recognized as her own but which came from somebody else burst from the kitchen. An instant later, she saw her own form rush into the room, carrying a wand. Sarah growled in anger at the sight of Melania wearing her face. Never had something more personal been stolen from her.

"Don't think I'm not prepared for you," Melania said with a hiss. She raised her wand defensively. Sarah's mom stepped forward, fists clenched as though she were going to attack Sarah with her bare hands. Kay, Keeley, and Carrie rushed in front of Sarah, forming a barrier in front of her.

"Wait!" Carrie called. "You need to know the truth!"

"Get out of the way, Carrie," Sarah's mom said. "You've obviously been put under Melania's spell. We can help you."

"Mom . . ." Sarah's voice was quiet and unfamiliar, but it still stopped everybody in their tracks. She pushed her way past her friends and stood within arm's reach of her mom. "Please hear me out. I know I don't always think before I act, and I know I tend to do dangerous things with my magic because of it, but I'm not going to do it here. Please . . ." She swallowed, trying to moisten a throat that felt extraordinarily dry. "Please listen to me, because I can't fight you. Even if I can't save you, I won't risk hurting you."

"Nice try," Melania said, "but we know your tricks. *Abeo confest—*"

"Stop." Sarah's mom grabbed Melania's arm, pushing the wand downward until it faced the floor.

Nobody moved in the silence that followed. Sarah's mom studied everybody closely, her eyes like two piercing blue lights. She smiled slightly when she noticed Keeley in her dragon-bunny form but otherwise kept a hard, grim expression on her face.

Finally, she locked eyes with Sarah. "Melania," she said firmly, "a mother knows her daughter. *Cadar coresto sidar!*"

She turned as she spoke those words, pointing her wand at the real Melania and catching her off-guard. The girl wearing Sarah's form tumbled backward as a green bolt of magical force struck her. Her wand fell from her grasp, and she let out a shout of pain as she hit the wall.

In the space of a single heartbeat, things returned to normal. In fact, they were better than normal. Sarah looked down at her hands and saw that they were truly her own. Melania's illusion had vanished, and she lay helplessly on the ground.

Melania lunged for Sarah's wand, but Sarah moved more swiftly, grabbing it first and pointing it at her foe. They'd been in this position before, but Sarah knew Melania wouldn't be able to pull the switch again now that all her friends were watching for such trickery.

"It makes no sense," Melania said, her voice wavering. The shadows in the corner of the home darkened, and the lights flickered as she spoke. "Everybody hates Melania. She's a mind-witch. A shadow-sorceress. But everybody loves Sarah, the second Emerald Enchantress. How can that change so quickly? Why did people trust you when you wore my form?"

She clenched her fists and pounded the floor in futility. The color drained out of her face, making her seem like she was nothing more than a china doll with blood-red lips.

"What kind of power do you have over these people?" Melania screamed.

"It's not power," Sarah replied.

Melania's lips curled back, and she snarled like an angry dog. Sarah tensed and prepared to blast her foe with a spell, but then she remembered that most dogs only attacked people if they were sick or scared. It occurred to her that Melania was probably both.

She felt the presence of her mom and her friends around her and knew she was strong because of them. Carrie, who had done her best to protect her even as a helpless captive. Kay, whose kind heart had spared her life even when he thought she was an enemy. Keeley, who recognized Sarah no matter what form she wore. Her mom, who took all of her complaints and arguments and met her with love and trust in return. And, of course, Dax, who'd willingly given his life to make sure she was safe.

Melania had nobody like that in her life, only shadows and people she tried to force into friendship. Sarah couldn't forgive her foe for what she'd done, but she also couldn't help but pity her.

She lowered her wand. Melania must have read the sadness on her face. That look of pity seemed to strike her worse than any spell that might've been launched her way. She shrieked as if something had torn her in two. Then, inexplicably, she began laughing.

"It doesn't matter, does it?" Melania said, cackling. "I'll never have what I want. I can't earn it, and I can't steal it. But I can still take your lives from you!"

The world around them twisted and shook. The walls bent and then burst open, revealing a void of shadow beyond. The roof above their heads flew off as though it had been seized by a hurricane, and a starless black sky looked down upon them. From every corner of newly-created shadow spilled forth dozens—if not hundreds—of shadow creatures. Some drew swords. Others held up razor sharp claws.

"Die," Melania said with a hiss. "All of you, just die."

The companions bunched together in a circle, facing insurmountable odds together one last time. Keeley hopped forward and breathed out a ball of fire, but for every shadow creature that got burned, two more stepped forward to take its place. Even as Carrie held her sword defensively, ready for yet another fight, Sarah could feel her friend shaking.

Sarah herself, however, felt uncommonly calm.

"Mom," she said, "this world's never seen what two Emerald Enchantresses can do."

Her mom nodded grimly. "You're right, sweetie. Let's show them."

The two enchantresses broke the defensive circle as the shadow creatures rushed them. Rather than cast their spells individually, Sarah and her mom crossed their wands. They looked into each other's eyes and let their feelings guide them. Words began tumbling from their lips. Sarah didn't even think about what spells she was casting—she just let her heart guide it.

The world of shadow suddenly lit up with a bright emerald light. Figures sprang forth from the two wands, each representing somebody the two enchantresses had met in their journeys through Greystone Valley. Dwarves, ogres, dragons, and fey sprang to life, creating an army of fantastic creatures that fought tooth and nail against the shadows.

Even with these emerald reinforcements, the fight seemed evenly matched. But then, another figure emerged from the combined might of their magic. Dax stepped forward like a green ghost, arcing his sword with the practiced ease that he always did. His blade burned with jade-colored fire. Wherever he struck, a shadowy figure vanished.

Sarah's eyes began to blur with tears as she realized that this was the only way she would ever see her old friend again. She blinked those tears back—she would shed them later. For now, she just whispered one last thank you to the old warrior as the last of Melania's shadows melted away.

In less than a minute, the phantoms and memories that Sarah and her mom had summoned vanished. But they had eliminated all of Melania's shadowy allies. Now, in the black void around them, there was only their single foe, and she found herself with Kay's staff and Carrie's sword pointed directly at her heart.

"How I would have loved to really be you instead of just a shadow." Melania sank to her knees and bowed her head, waiting for the killing blow.

"You're not a shadow," Sarah said. "But you should know by now that shadows and lies aren't going to make you friends."

"I'll never have any friends. I'll never have any life. Greystone Valley was my last hope."

"What do we do with her now?" Kay asked. "Even if we bring her back to Greystone Valley for a trial, there's no prison that can hold a witch this powerful."

Sarah made a mental list of the spells she could call forth to end the problem right now. She could burn Melania to ash or turn her to stone. She had wished for the strength to finally finish her off, but now she could only think of a different, more impressive kind of strength—the kind her friends had shown her when she was trapped in a cage and they had no reason to believe her words. When she was truly helpless, her friends had shown mercy . . . a power her spells alone couldn't duplicate.

A bell sounded in Sarah's mind as she recalled her time in that cage. "There is a cage that can hold her," she said. "I was in one just a few hours ago."

Melania gave a dry laugh that sounded like dying leaves. "So I'm to be a prisoner? Locked away for the rest of my life? I suppose you find some irony in this, don't you, Carrie?"

"Not really," Carrie said. "When you made me a prisoner, I hadn't committed a crime. And we're not going to try to force you to be somebody's friend. You might be behind bars for a long time, but you'll still have your life. And maybe—just maybe—you'll see the error of your ways and make a real change."

"Ha," Melania said humorlessly. "What a world that would be."

"There's one other option," Sarah said. "We could leave here and seal the door to this world, make sure you never leave it again. But I think you'd rather be in a place where you're not alone, whether it's a jail or not. We won't keep the cell a secret. People will talk to you and care for you. It will give you time—time to stop hating yourself and see past all the shadows you've put in your way."

Sarah extended her hand toward her defeated foe. After a very long moment, Melania took it.

Twenty-Nine

"The school has brought me in as a temporary replacement for Mr. Daxon," Dr. Goldberg said. "He seems to have disappeared completely, and I understand he called you into his office shortly before that. Did he say anything strange to you?"

"Lots," Sarah said.

Dr. Goldberg folded his wrinkled hands together and leaned so far forward that his chin nearly touched to top of his cluttered desk. "What did he say, Sarah?"

Sarah sighed. Days had passed since she and Carrie had returned home from Greystone Valley. Life had gone on just as it had before, except perhaps with a better understanding between her and her mom. But now she found herself back in the same situation she had been in before: a whole world of magic lay right under everybody's nose, but she couldn't show it to them.

"Sarah? You haven't started daydreaming again, have you?"

Dr. Goldberg was a small, bald man with a gray mustache and glasses that seemed too big for his face. Sarah met him over a year ago, back when her mom was worried that she couldn't tell the difference between fantasy and reality—and back when Sarah didn't realize that sometimes they were one and the same.

His office, temporary though it may be, was already filled with more books and papers than Dax's had been. He must've shaken his head when he came in to find how sparse "Mr. Daxon's" library was and how little he interacted with the students. As far as anybody in this world knew, Dax would be remembered as a quaint old man who never did his job and disappeared without a trace.

Knowing how little of the truth Dr. Goldberg would believe, Sarah's eyes glittered mischievously as she leaned forward in her chair. "Do you really want to know about him?"

"Yes, please."

"Well first of all, his name wasn't Mr. Daxon. It was Dax, and he came here from a place called Greystone Valley. He was the thirteenth son of the thirteenth son, as gloomy as you can ever imagine, but he had the best sword arm in any world there ever was. He also cared more about his friends than anybody I've ever met. He traveled from another world so he could restore my memory and help overthrow the witch who conquered Greystone Valley. With nothing but a sword and some courage, he faced Grimjaw the dragon in single combat and slew him. The battle cost him his life, but he got a hero's burial and will always be known as the greatest swordsman that world has ever seen. And no matter what gets said about him here, his true friends will never forget him."

Dr. Goldberg's face flushed red. Sarah grinned in satisfaction as he took a moment to compose himself.

"Young lady," he huffed, "I don't know what I expected out of you, but with a matter as serious as this, I thought you would have enough respect not to start telling more of your stories again."

Sarah stood up from her chair and made a mock curtsy. "I have to get back to class now, sir. But don't worry, my mom is already expecting a call from you."

While Dr. Goldberg sputtered and stammered, she left his office and continued on with her day.

"I've got a dance recital on Monday," Carrie said as she walked with Sarah on her way home. "Not that you care, but—"

"I'll be there," Sarah said.

Carrie looked genuinely shocked. "Really?"

"Sure. You let yourself stay locked in a cell for me. The least I could do . . ." She shook her head and tried to start over. "Um, not that I think a dance recital is the same as a jail sentence. It's . . . I'm . . ."

"I think I know what you mean."

"Who knows?" Sarah said. "I might even like it—just a little bit, mind you."

"You really don't have to."

"No, I don't," Sarah said. "That's the idea."

After a while of walking in silence, Carrie started a new line of conversation. "You know, I definitely don't want to run through dank tunnels and fight monsters, but I feel like I kind of missed out a little. You got to see the countryside, and I spent most of my time locked in a tower. And there wasn't even good food there!"

"Would you rather have been poisoned and beaten up by gremlins?" Sarah asked.

"Well, obviously not. But there's got to be a nice, happy medium, right? I mean, Greystone Valley can't always be at the mercy of a warlord or evil witch, can it? There's got to be some times when a person can just enjoy the scenery and maybe fly on a dragon's back."

"We wouldn't be able to fit on Keeley's back, and the rest of the dragons live in hiding."

Carrie grinned. "Well, it would be fun to look for them, wouldn't it?"

Sarah kicked some dry autumn leaves into the gutter. Her house sat on the horizon, and the sky was gray behind it. Maybe if it started to thunder, she could do some storm chasing tonight . . .

The last few days had found her quiet and thoughtful, trying to find a lesson she could take out of what she'd experienced. Instead, she found frustration over the fact that nobody in this world except for herself, her mom, and Carrie would ever really understand Dax's sacrifice.

And she also felt a little angry, because Greystone Valley only seemed to summon her when it needed help. It wasn't fair that she didn't get a choice as to when she got to visit the mystical land. Not that she wasn't happy to be home, but . . .

"I'd like to go back again," she said. "Just to visit."

"Well, why not just find the spell that brings us back?"

"It's not in my spellbook. I asked my mom, and it's not in hers either. It seems to be something Kay cooked up through that muddled way of spellcasting he has." Sarah snorted and stomped her foot. "He's got to be the worst wizard in the world who also happens to be the best."

"He stayed in the valley to make sure Melania got locked away properly. He's there, and we're here, so I guess that's that." Carrie made a funny-sounding sigh, as though she were trying to hold back laughter.

Sarah raised a curious eyebrow toward her friend but didn't press any further. They reached the front door of her house, and she threw it open, kicking off her shoes and calling to her mom once she got inside.

"I'm in the living room, darling," her mom responded.

"So, do you have any plans for this weekend?" Carried asked as she followed Sarah into the house.

"No," Sarah said, "but it seems like you do."

"I'm taking a trip," Carrie said.

"Is that right?"

They stepped into the living room, and the conversation ground to a halt. Sitting on the couch, just as he had been about a week ago, was Kay. His clothes still didn't fit him right, but he wore an oversized hooded sweater and ragged sneakers instead of usual baggy robes.

"Yes," he said, finishing the conversation that had gone on between Sarah and Carrie. "That's right."

It took Sarah a moment to find her voice. "Is there trouble in Greystone Valley again?" she finally asked.

"No," Kay said. "It just took Keeley and I a bit to get things back in order. I had to miss some days of school, and now I'm way behind on studying for my math test on Monday, so if anything, the trouble's here."

Sarah furrowed her brow. "Why would you leave your whole world behind just to take a math test?"

Kay scratched the back of his neck. "Because that's where you two are, of course."

"But it's Friday now, and the test isn't until Monday," Carrie said.

Sarah's face lit up. "You knew Kay was back? Your trip is back to Greystone Valley?"

"Surprise," Carrie said.

"Keeley and I wanted to show the two of you Firkrag Forest, where there may not be any fire-breathing bunnies, but there do happen to be some very friendly talking trees."

Sarah cast a glance at her mom. "I did all my chores this morning, and I don't have much homework . . ."

Her mom sighed. "Stay away from gremlins, and be sure to get word to me if anything world shaking comes up."

Sarah hugged her mom, then rushed over to Kay's side as he began to cast his spell.

"When we get to the other side, be sure to count all your fingers and toes," she told Carrie.

In a flash, the friends disappeared.

Afterword

My wife, Sarah Brooks, remains a driving force behind her namesake's adventures in Greystone Valley, and she proved invaluable in the writing of this sequel.

My mother, Pat Brooks, died of cancer before this book could reach shelves and is dearly missed. Nonetheless, her spirit is present here even as she joins my father, Ronald Brooks, in the afterlife.

This series continues to owe a great debt to many fantasy classics, especially the works of Lloyd Alexander. This time around, the influence of the late, great Terry Pratchett was an especially noteworthy influence, with my feeble homage to his humor and wit showing through here and there.

Many thanks to everybody who provided feedback on Greystone Valley, which helped strengthen this sequel, and to Grey Gecko Press for making it possible. And, as always, kudos to Jessica Von Braun for her terrific art.

Support Indie Authors & Small Press

If you liked this book, please take a few moments to leave a review on your favorite website, even if it's only a line or two. Reviews make all the difference to indie authors and are one of the best ways you can help support our work.

Reviews on Amazon, GreyGeckoPress.com, GoodReads, Barnes and Noble, or even on your own blog or website all help to spread the word to more readers about our books, and nothing's better than word-of-mouth!

http://smarturl.it/review-conquest

About the Author

Charlie Brooks is a lifelong resident of Vermont who fell in love with fantasy literature at a young age. *Conquest of Greystone Valley* marks his first sequel, following up on Sarah's original adventure in *Greystone Valley*.

He is a finalist in Season 9 of Paizo Publishing's RPG Superstar, the winner of the 2006 Chaffin Award for Fiction ("Fantasy As You Like It"), and the co-winner of the 2011 New Millennium Writings Fiction Prize ("Eight-Bit Heaven").

Conquest of Greystone Valley draws inspiration from fantasy stories ranging from *The Chronicles of Prydain* to the *Discworld* series. Most importantly, it is a tale for Charlie's wife Sarah and his children Quentin and Cordelia, who bring a bit of fantasy into everyday life.

Connect with Charlie

Email:	chmbrooks@gmail.com
Facebook:	facebook.com/chmbrooks
Web:	chbrooks.com

Grey Gecko Press

Thank you for reading this book from Grey Gecko Press, an independent publishing company bringing you great books by your favorite new indie authors.

Be one of the first to hear about new releases from Grey Gecko: visit our website and sign up for our New Release or All-Access email lists. Don't worry: we hate spam, too. You'll only be notified when there's a new release, we'll never share your email with anyone for any reason, and you can unsubscribe at any time.

At our website you can purchase all our titles, including special and autographed editions, preorder upcoming books, and find out about two great ways to get free books, the Slushpile Reader Program and the Advance Reader Program.

And don't forget: all our print editions come with the ebook free!

More from Charlie Brooks

Greystone Valley

by Charlie Brooks

Greystone Valley is a land of wizards, dragons, and warriors—and one young girl who goes there quite by accident when her idle wish is granted.

Sarah discovers that not everything in the valley is as magic as she might've wished—especially the nearly illiterate wizard, the mouse-sized dragon, and the warrior who can't stand the sight of blood. Being hunted isn't helping, either. Will Sarah survive this new life of hers, and can she make it home?

And, more importantly, can she ever be the same again?

amazon **iBooks**

BARNES&NOBLE BOOKSELLERS **kobo**

grey gecko press

http://bit.ly/1ehaBL8

Recommended Reading

Horse
by Leon Berger

This bittersweet chronicle of a working horse finally gaining his freedom was inspired by a real animal and true events, yet its underlying theme is about the universal value of friendship.

The hero is a sturdy draft horse: old, eccentric, and irritable. His name, suitably enough, is Groucho. By day, he hauls a tourist carriage around the heritage streets of Montreal. By night, he goes home to a stable in a run-down, working-class district.

When his owner dies, Groucho feels the loss and is helped through it by the ancient stableman, Doyle, who is also set in his ways. This is the story of how they cope with each other, as well as the threat which endangers their entire way of life.

amazon **iBooks**
BARNES&NOBLE BOOKSELLERS **kobo**

grey gecko press
http://bit.ly/141V9lW

A Wing and a Prayer
by John Morano

Lupé might be the very last Guadalupe petrel alive, and he knows the best way to save his flock is to find the Islands of Life and a mate. The problem is the well-meaning man-flock that's decided to keep him safe . . . in a cage. But Lupé has hatched an escape plan all his own!

Told in a 'Disneyesque' style, *A Wing and a Prayer* will have you smiling and laughing as you're introduced to wonderful characters but also important themes, especially the environment.

Often compared to works such as *Jonathan Livingston Seagull*, *Watership Down*, and *The Jungle Books*, this 25th Anniversary Edition also features an introduction by Mark Tercek, President and CEO of The Nature Conservancy.

amazon **iBooks**
BARNES&NOBLE BOOKSELLERS **kobo**

grey gecko press
http://bit.ly/1YmKfQq

www.ingramcontent.com/pod-product-compliance
Lightning Source LLC
Chambersburg PA
CBHW060545190726
48283CB00003B/874